THE DREAM KING

THE DREAM KING

BY GREGOR ROBINSON

Porcepic Books
an imprint of

Beach Holme Publishing
Vancouver

This book is published by Beach Holme Publishing, #226—2040 West 12th Ave., Vancouver, BC, V6J 2G2. This is a Porcepic Book.

We acknowledge the generous assistance of The Canada Council and the BC Ministry of Small Business, Tourism and Culture.

THE CANADA COUNCIL FOR THE ARTS SINCE 1957   LE CONSEIL DES ARTS DU CANADA DEPUIS 1957

Editor: Joy Gugeler
Production and Design: Teresa Bubela, Joy Gugeler

Cover Art: *Birthday (l'Anniversaire)* by Marc Chagall, 1915, oil on cardboard, 31.25 x 39.25", Museum of Modern Art, New York, acquired through Lillie P. Bliss Bequest. Photograph © 1997 The Museum of Modern Art, New York.

Canadian Cataloguing in Publication Data:

Robinson, Gregor
    The dream king

(A Porcepic Book)
ISBN 0-88878-377-9

    I. Title. II. Series.

PS8585.O351625D74 1997   C813'.54   C97-900647-3
PR9199.3.R5338D74 1997

FOR MY MOTHER AND MY FATHER

CONTENTS

◇ ◇ ◇ ◇

GAPS

◇ ◇ ◇ ◇

In the eyes of his parents, Dearborn lived in a foreign country and it made him feel like an alien. How on earth would he tell them about Helen? He thought of himself as dutiful—he phoned his mother every Sunday and there were even occasional letters—but there was always reproach. Why had he left his home town? Dearborn said that this was life in the Twentieth Century. People left towns and homes in the country and moved to cities. People were in motion, not only in Ontario (he had only moved one hundred seventy miles, after all; they ought to put the matter in perspective) but across the globe. There was greed, fear, hatred, starvation; immense economic and demographic forces were at work. Dearborn knew these things. He earned a living doing market research, was an expert in his field.

That was another thing. "What is it you do, dear?" his mother would say. "People ask—your Aunt Adelle, friends—and I'm never able to explain. Not advertising, I know that. But something. What, exactly? What do you *do*?"

His father had been a bank manager, as had his father

1

before him.

They were arriving that afternoon, staying three or four days. Dearborn had the details before him—his mother's clear handwriting on blue letterhead with a line drawing of the house where both he and his father had been raised. His grandmother had moved next door; his mother visited her every day until she died. His parents' lives made Dearborn feel insubstantial, like the cotton that drifted from the branches of the big trees that grew at the end of lawn.

They were coming to visit the children, his mother wrote. They thought it would be a help. They didn't know that "the difficulty", as his mother always called it, was long over, had all been settled, really, the first year of the marriage.

And his father would visit doctors. He was being watched. For diabetes. For the arthritis that interfered with his walks. He also drank too much. "Eight ounces a day, I said to the doctor!" he'd told Dearborn the last time he was in the city, his eyes bright. His heart. And the thing they avoided— his spells.

"Stupid!" Roxanne shouted. Dearborn looked up from his mother's letter, working the gap in his teeth with his tongue. "Careless girl!" Roxanne shouted. It was an expression of Anne's. Dearborn used to admonish her, "Don't speak to the children like that. They'll pick it up."

"Girls," he yelled "stop yelling."

"The reason they're always yelling," Anne would tell him, "is because you're always yelling. You should listen to yourself sometime."

"We're not fighting," Roxanne yelled back from the living room. She was the older one, almost six. Jasmine was three and a half, and in her current phase preferred to be called Snow White. Jasmine and Roxanne.

"What kind of a name is Jasmine?" Dearborn's mother had asked. "Are there Arabs in our family somewhere? Am I missing something?"

Roxanne and Jasmine. Anne's choices. Dearborn would have named them Mary and Susan. One of the many decisions over which he had *not* exercised his veto.

The latest thing was that Anne wanted one of the girls. She didn't see how splitting them up made any difference, since they were adopted anyway. He said it was creepy, and it was crazy. They were supposed to be a family.

"But we aren't a family any more," said Anne. "You and that teenager."

"She's not a teenager," he'd told her. "And you started it." Almost true, Dearborn reflected. We order events according to our own mythologies.

Roxanne, walking around now with one of the fat lamps in her arms: "It's alright, Sarah," she said to the lamp. "I'm here. Daddy's here."

"What are you playing?" Dearborn asked.

"Big sister. This is the baby. Her name's Sarah."

"I told you, don't play with the lamps. Use a doll, the cat, something. You drop this lamp, you'll cut yourself."

"Is it made of china?"

"It's made of china. You know that," said Dearborn.

"It's precious, right?"

"Precious. Very precious, but not as precious as you." It was a discussion they'd had before. "Plus you could electrocute yourself pulling the plug."

Dearborn took the lamp and put it back on the table. He handed her one of the dolls from the armchair. But she'd already picked up the bookends, budgies in white marble. "It's alright, Sarah, don't cry," she said to one of the bookends. "Do you want to go to sleep? It's alright, you go to sleep. I'll be right here in the next room. I'll wear my big shoes, so you'll be able to hear me walking."

There was a note from the senior kindergarten teacher attached to the refrigerator door with a Pizza Hut magnet: *Please make a special effort to come on Monday. We would like to talk about Roxanne.*

Roxanne came into the kitchen. "Daddy, are you going to marry Helen?"

Dearborn shrugged, his mouth full of muffin.

"Moon and June and kissing," said Roxanne. "Yuck."

She turned and left, back to the living room, where Jasmine was playing with the cassette machine.

"Daddy, show us your monster laugh." Jasmine had sneaked up behind him through the dining room door.

During an argument on their first anniversary, Anne had reached across the glass table (they had crammed her patio furniture onto the tiny balcony of their 21st floor apartment) and slapped Dearborn so hard she loosened an old tooth. Now he had a crown, cloned on some fragment of the actual tooth. It kept falling out. He couldn't afford to go to the dentist every time, so he endured the gap, did the monster laugh. On special occasions—nights out, meetings with clients—he shoved the tooth in with some chewing gum. It was usually good for two, perhaps three hours.

Roxanne came in with a tangerine. She wanted Dearborn

to do Marlon Brando from *The Godfather*, another of his specialities.

"Not today, girls. The monster has a headache."

"You and Helen had too much wine, right Daddy?"

Dearborn led them into the living room and put *The Three Stooges* on the video.

"How could you have bought that for them?" Anne had asked. "You think its funny, hitting people over the head, sticking things up nostrils? You want them to grow up like that?"

Dearborn did think it was funny. And he hadn't grown up like that. *What about your mother?* he thought. *She thinks farts are funny.* Dearborn was at the stage where he was still framing responses, composing ripostes to old jabs.

Upstairs, Helen was sitting on the floor in the corner of the bedroom, playing with the cat. She was just out of the bathroom. She was wearing bikini underpants, no top.

"I love you," Dearborn told her. He bent down and kissed her left nipple. She smelled of his shower soap. "But you have to move your things out of the house."

She shrugged her shoulders. "You're forty-four, right? Maybe it's time to tell them. Your parents. You know, like, you have a penis? You like girls?"

"You're only twenty-four. My mother is seventy-two."

"Great. Now we know everybody's age."

"They haven't taken it in that Anne is out of the picture. They think we might get back together."

"Doesn't matter to me. Really. I just think you should level with them. I don't believe in shame."

"It's not a question of shame," said Dearborn. "I just don't want them to know I'm involved so soon after my wife has left. And with a woman twenty years younger."

"Like it might give them the wrong idea? I think they're old enough, you know?"

"How about *your* mother?" Dearborn asked. "What does she think about us?"

"She likes you. She does. After Anne first left, she wanted to ask you over for dinner. She wanted to go out with you herself. I think so. I really do. Get you in the sack."

"What about the age difference?"

"She's only two years older than you."

It wasn't just his imagination: he and Helen always seemed to be talking about people's ages. "I meant the difference between you and me," he said.

Helen's mother was on her own; her husband had just come out. "We used to wonder, like, why he never came home?" Helen had told Dearborn and Anne when she'd first found out. "Those walks in the park?"

"Another homo," Anne had said, glaring at Dearborn. She was at the stage where she still blamed everything on man, the species. She was always in the process of escaping a world of vile men.

Dearborn took Helen by the hand and pulled her up, towards the bed.

"I've got class today," Helen said.

She taught classes at a gym, Saturday mornings. Dearborn told her he would give her a lift. Anne had left him the car. He'd won that argument—he needed the car for his work. In the end, when Anne moved out, Dearborn had quit his job and gone freelance. He now hated being out of the house, hated being away from the children. He stayed at home with the kids and his modem, Helen and teenagers from the neighbourhood helping out with the sitting. But he still had the car.

Before she got out, Helen said, "Warren called again."

Her ex-boyfriend. Warren Blue (he had invented his own name) played bass in a bar band. Otherwise, he did nothing. Dearborn would sometimes notice him loitering on the sidewalk in front of the house. Warren's career allowed plenty of time for watching and besetting. It was hard for Dearborn to understand how Helen had ever become involved with such a person. She said it had started when she was in her freshman year, when she hadn't had the confidence to say no. Warren Blue was six foot three. No doubt he was tireless in bed, thought Dearborn.

"Won't take no for an answer," he said.

"Won't take an answer, period," said Helen. "Bass players are strange."

Dearborn took this as some kind of message, a vague threat. "I'll tell my parents about us soon," he said. "Perhaps, before they go home."

"See you tonight."

"Where are we going?" Dearborn's father asked. He gazed around the hall. He had just left the TV room. He wore an old tweed jacket with saggy pockets. His glasses were crooked.

"Maple Leaf Gardens," said Dearborn.

"Don't see why," said his father. "Don't see why we have

to go out."

"Jack, try to fit in," said Dearborn's mother. She held his coat over her arm, waiting.

"You used to like hockey," Dearborn said.

"He still likes hockey," said his mother. "He watches on television all the time."

"Matlock was just starting," said his father, vaguely affronted. He shuffled along to the bathroom. From the hallway, Dearborn and his mother heard the click of the lock. They heard him urinate. They heard a gurgling sound. Dearborn's father kept a bottle in his shaving kit.

"One good thing," said Dearborn's mother. "He's drinking less. He forgets where he puts it. He forgets that he likes it."

His father opened the bathroom door. He positively beamed. "Hockey!" he said. "They've finally started to win."

Downstairs, Helen was waiting. She was dressed in faded jeans and a black ribbed turtle neck. Her hair was glossy. She was babysitting the children.

"I'm glad to meet you at last. I've heard so much about you," Helen said when Dearborn introduced her to his parents.

"You have?" said his mother, glancing at Dearborn. She had eyes like a hawk.

After the game, Dearborn took them out for a coffee. The restaurant was brightly lit with huge orange globes, illuminating the brown and orange decor. The place was crowded and the manager sat them at a big table with a father and two young boys. The boys looked remarkably like their father, Dearborn noticed. As he aged, he took note of family resemblance more and more. He was becoming something of an expert on nature versus nurture, the various theories. What effect would divorce have on his children, he wondered?

The two boys had souvenir programmes from the game spread on the table.

"Good game," said Dearborn's father, smiling at them.

The boys nodded.

"I used to play for the Leafs," said Dearborn's father.

Was this true, Dearborn wondered? His father had played for McGill, before the war, and Dearborn remembered something about him having been asked to try out for the pros. But nothing more, surely.

"Yeah?" said the older boy. He would have been about nine. "Wicked," said the younger, about six.

"Yup," said Dearborn's father. "Played with Eddie Shore and Turk Broda. Teeter Kennedy."

The boys' father looked at Dearborn's father in studied silence. The boys were silent too. Perhaps the way Dearborn and his mother were watching, waiting to see what would happen next, gave them a signal.

"Johnny Bower. Gordie Howe. All the greats," said Dearborn's father.

"Johnny Bower?" said the older boy, puzzled.

"Really," said the father. He definitely knew now that the chronology was impossible. He was young, maybe twenty-eight. Dearborn noticed that he had the same kind of intonation, used the same expressions as Helen.

"When did Gordie Howe play for the Leafs?" the older boy asked his father. "Gordie Howe never played for the

Leafs."

"Eat your cake," the father answered.

"Is that guy weird, or what?" asked the six year old, half whispering.

Dearborn's father looked down at his coffee. He took off his glasses; his eyes were red-rimmed. Dearborn thought his father might weep, and he reached out and put his hand on his arm.

"I think I'll go downstairs and have a pee," said his father, with immense dignity. Dearborn and his mother watched him shamble towards the kitchen. He looked up at the clock on the wall, stopped, then kept on towards the kitchen door. The boys beside them watched too, clearly fascinated by a man who got lost in a restaurant.

"I think you'd better go with him," said Dearborn's mother.

On the way home, she sat in the front seat, talking about the town where Dearborn had grown up, people he had known when he was a child.

"You heard about Henry Rollins," she said, looking at him sideways. "He's up at Penetang, locked up. He was in a variety store. He fell asleep standing at the magazine rack. That's what he does, you know—falls asleep standing up. Happens all the time. When the owner woke him up, Henry stabbed him. So the police came and they took him up to Penetang." Henry Rollins was Dearborn's age. He was adopted.

After a few moments silence, Dearborn's mother said, "It's not Helen, is it?"

"It's not Helen what? She babysits."

"Old to be a babysitter," said his mother.

"Not that old."

"Not that old—you're right about that. She can't be more than twenty-five."

In the rearview mirror Dearborn saw his father put his finger in his ear and shake it with a vigour that made Dearborn wonder how he didn't dislodge his own yellow teeth. His mother noticed too; she turned and gave Dearborn a look. The finger-in-ear business—it was a sign, a warning flag in their family. Dearborn's father did not like discussions about personal matters. He preferred undercurrents.

"Good God," he said, looking out the window. "Do you see?"

"What?" said Dearborn's mother.

"The people. Where are we? Africa? Pakistan? Where do they come from? Why do we let them in? Used to be a perfectly good country."

"You and Anne, you should never have moved down here," said Dearborn's mother, ignoring this diversion.

"Mother, grow up."

"I'm seventy-two. How much more grown up do want me?" She sighed heavily. "Alright, I can accept this divorce business, although I never thought we'd have it in our family. Perhaps now you'll have children of your own." Her family had been in Ontario since the American Revolution.

Dearborn glanced up and caught his father looking at him in the mirror. There was a momentary bright look in his eyes; he was with them again, had broken through the haze of whisky, the floating cobwebs, the ganglions in his brain.

He said, "He already has his own children. Bonny children they are, too."

They drove the rest of the way in silence. When Dearborn

pulled into the driveway, his father said, "You have a garage?" He knew perfectly well they had a garage. Dearborn had parked the car there when he'd brought them back from the bus station.

"I would like to see the garage," said his father.

"Don't tell him how to get into the garage," said Dearborn's mother under her breath.

"Door halfway down the basement stairs," said Dearborn. His father nodded, turned to shuffle up the front steps. He would be getting something from his shaving kit, a stash to hide in the garage for the duration of the visit. He kept bottles in the garage at home. Wherever he went he liked to establish a safe haven. Dearborn's mother glared at him, and Dearborn was suddenly enraged again. This was a recent phenomenon, the rage that seemed to come in waves.

Dearborn said to his mother, "If he wants a drink he can have one."

The truth was his father didn't actually drink that much any more, certainly less than Dearborn. He simply liked the routines, the hiding of bottles and so on, and Dearborn understood that.

On Monday evening Dearborn stood before the bathroom mirror, affixing his tooth in the gap with a big wad of gum in preparation for the visit to the school. He could hear the television from the den along the hall where his parents were watching the six o'clock news. Then he heard different noises. Someone entering the house. Could it be Helen, ignoring his warning? The door from the porch closed quietly. The footsteps stopped. Intruders! Teenagers, no doubt. Dearborn's heart raced. He poked his head in the door of the den. His parents sat staring at the television; they had heard nothing. He told them he was going to check the casserole. He crept down the stairs.

It was only Warren Blue, six foot three and skinny as a rail, standing in the middle of the kitchen. He wore a greasy buckskin jacket that hung shapelessly from his shoulders. "Where's Helen?" Warren stepped towards Dearborn, as though he were going to push by him and make his way upstairs to the bedroom. He looked angry. His face was blotchy.

Dearborn said, "No need to get riled up."

"Fuck you," said Warren.

Upstairs, there was a stirring, Dearborn's father on one of his trips to the bathroom. Then his mother's shoes along the hall floor. Her footsteps grew silent, muffled as she descended the carpeted stairs. Weren't they supposed to be hard of hearing?

"She's not here, Warren. I'm sorry. I think she said something about an aerobics class. If I see her, I'll tell her you're looking for her. Listen, I have guests. I think you'd better go."

Dearborn made a move toward the back door, to show him out. Warren grabbed Dearborn's arm, twisted him around and slapped him across the face, as though Dearborn were a cheeky school girl. Dearborn's hand shot out in a reflex movement, a light shove to Warren's chest. Warren responded with a real punch, a blow to Dearborn's mouth that nearly knocked him off his feet. He tasted salty blood and salty tears. The tears were not tears of emotion, nor tears of rage; they welled up involuntarily with the pain. He felt the gap in his teeth with his tongue. His mouth was filling with blood.

Suddenly the room was full of people. His parents hovering behind him—it appeared that they could move quickly and quietly when they wanted to—the children up from the basement, and Helen bobbing behind Warren in the back door.

Roxanne said, "Daddy, are you going to need a needle?"

Jasmine saw the blood and began to cry.

Dearborn said, "Mother, Dad, this is Warren Blue, a neighbour of ours. And Helen, you know Helen of course."

"The babysitter," said Dearborn's father. "Delighted to see you again. Are we going out?"

"I've seen you walking up and down the sidewalk in front of the house," Dearborn's mother said to Warren Blue.

Warren and Helen looked at each other. She put her arm on his back, running her hand up underneath his buckskin jacket. She seemed to whisper something, calm him down. Then he turned, her fingers grazing along his back as they walked through the door.

Dearborn knew then he would not have to face the problem of how to tell his parents about Helen. She was going back to Warren. It was simply a matter of when.

"That was something," his father said. "Never seen a fight before."

"Very stupid," said his mother. "You're far too old for this sort of thing."

It was true; he was too old. But his father was wrong—it wasn't a fight. It was Dearborn standing there, and Warren hitting him in the mouth. It was as though it had happened to someone else.

His mother appeared with a wet washcloth. When

Dearborn examined himself in the mirror, he saw that blood was coming from the gap where he had jammed the tooth in. Usually when it came loose, he caught the tooth rolling around in his mouth, an immense foreign object. This time it was gone. He phoned the dentist, a neighbour, who told him to stuff a piece of cotton batting into the gap. The flow of blood would likely stop in a few minutes. Dearborn asked him about the tooth.

"This, too, will pass," said Dr. More.

"What?"

"You probably swallowed it. You could sift through, you know, after you go to the toilet."

"Absolutely not. Out of the question," Dearborn told him.

"At least a thousand bucks to do a new one and put it in," said Dr. More.

Dearborn would live with the gap. He cleaned himself up. He left his parents in front of the television, eating the casserole.

The school evening was set up so the children could greet parents at the door and show them around. There were big scrap books filled with drawings, scraggly numbers and alphabets. Then the pictures. The teacher would add the titles afterwards. ("What's this a picture of, sweetie?" "Daddy playing monster.")

Ms. Fish, the efficient one, was there by the desk to greet him. Tall, about thirty-eight, red hair done up with elaborate clips. The old friendly one, Mrs. Wesley, stood a few feet behind, clasping her hands. She reminded Dearborn of his grandmother. She hugged the children when they arrived in the morning.

Ms. Fish took him aside. "Will your wife be joining us?"

"No," said Dearborn.

"Yes," said Anne. She came hurrying toward them, wispy blonde hair plastered across her forehead.

"What are you doing here?" said Dearborn.

"They called me about Roxanne."

"Why would they call you?"

"Roxanne talks to things," said Ms. Fish, quiet and solicitous.

The wave came again. Dearborn was enraged. He listened to his wife and Ms. Fish talking about Roxanne. He grabbed Ms. Fish by the wrist. He could feel the heat in his face. No doubt the vein in his forehead was sticking out.

Anne said, "Jack, take it easy. It's not serious, only mild troubles, they said."

"Mrs. Fish," said Dearborn, still holding her by the arm.

"Ms.," said Ms. Fish.

"Mrs. Fish," said Dearborn, "I am aware that Roxanne talks to things. I live with her. She talks to lamps. She talks to bookends. She calls them Sarah. I am her father. I talk to things myself."

Other conversations in the room stopped.

"Mrs. Fish." Should he tell her everything, that the girl's mother had left despite her presence here tonight, that Roxanne was adopted, that he'd swallowed his tooth, that his father became lost on the way to the washroom in restaurants? Should he tell her about the inevitability of Helen and Warren Blue? "Mrs. Fish." Dearborn was aware that he was speaking through clenched teeth. "Do not speak of psychologists and professionals in front of my child."

"Oh God," said Anne.

Dearborn turned; he picked up the children at the play-dough table and fled from the room. In the parking lot, they sat in the dark car, waiting for the windshield to clear. He was exhausted. He was half asleep. His legs ached. His gap ached.

Roxanne said, "Daddy, what are you thinking?"

He didn't tell her. He was watching himself walking around the house, talking to the fat lamp, sifting through his own waste for a forty year old tooth.

On the radio, they were playing some kind of torch music.

Roxanne said, "Hey, hot lips." It was a mystery to Dearborn where these expressions came from. There was a new one every day.

"Poo-poo head," said Jasmine.

"Girls," said Dearborn, in warning.

Roxanne said, "Daddy, can I be the man of the house?"

"Who makes the hardest hugs?" said Jasmine, hugging him.

"Who makes the softest hugs?" said Roxanne, also hugging him. They sat like that, tangled in the front seat of the car.

HOW TO TALK ABOUT
WHAT HAPPENED

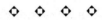

In early May, Dawn's therapist, the therapist from the Crisis Centre, said to Gordon, "You'll learn how to help, how to talk about what happened," but he never did.

◇ ◇ ◇ ◇

Gordon had met Dawn the previous fall, when the leaves from the maple trees that ringed the campus were yellow and red and crinkled underfoot, when the nights were still warm. She was in his evening class. She often did aerobics at the Athletics Centre first, and she would arrive on those smoky nights with her cheeks bright from the exercise, her hair dark and glossy, almost iridescent. These were the things that Gordon noticed.

She also did her studying at nights, because she had a full time job during the day. Because she found it so difficult to study at home, with the children in the house, she often went to the library after class and did her studying there.

A full-time job, the aerobics class, night school—and it was a full credit course—then an hour or so at the library. (Dawn told Gordon that she was hoping to get her degree eventually.) But all the time, in the back of her mind, fleeting thoughts of the children. She would be exhausted after a day like that. She would be less alert than she ought to be. Gordon understood that. All the same, he wished that she had been more careful. She ought to have stayed by the library's main door, bathed in the yellow light of the lobby where the commissionaire sat, until the bus arrived.

One moonless November night when the streets were slick with dead leaves and the temperature was dropping, Gordon drove Dawn home to her apartment in the east end. Twice before he had taken her out for coffee after class, but she had always made her own way home. She lived on the top floor of an old house on a ridge above a small ravine. You could see the railroad tracks from her bedroom. Through the bare branches of those autumn trees, you could see Lake Ontario. Dawn said that on some nights, late, after the traffic and the street cars on Queen Street had stopped, and when there was a particular kind of wind blowing, you could hear the muffled crash of waves on the shore. All his life in the city, Gordon had never been to an apartment or a house where you could actually see the lake from the windows. Like Dawn, it enchanted him.

The address book. That was what Dawn worried about most of all. She had written the children's names on some lined pages marked "Notes" inside the back cover, along with their sizes, and a list of the clothes they would need for the spring. She often wrote lists of things she needed; she would buy them later when she came across them at a good price. She had to be careful about money.

The address book was missing. Dawn would awaken suddenly in the middle of the night, thinking of these details in the address book: Kelly's birthday, Kelly's shoe size (Kelly had a wide foot for a four year old, she would be a good athlete some day), the name of Morgan's hockey coach, the name and address of the babysitter. (Gordon said to her, "But would anyone who didn't know already realize that it was the name of a sitter?") There was also a list of other, occasional sitters— young girls from the neighbourhood.

Dawn used to love those nights when the traffic stopped and the wind blew and she could hear the lake from her bedroom. Now she thought it was the lake that awakened her. She thought she might have to move to a new apartment, a highrise perhaps, with a doorman and security system. "Relax," Gordon would tell her. Irritated, he would rub the back of her neck. He wished he had never given her the address book.

Gordon rarely spent the whole night at Dawn's house. Before, it was because she didn't want him there in the morning when the children got up (he found this old-fashioned and charming). After, it was because she simply preferred that he not be there. She preferred to sleep with Kelly, either in her own bed, or in Kelly's room, in the upper bunk. She liked to look down from time to time at the peaceful expression on

Kelly's face. The sound of Kelly's breathing relaxed her, and she would be able to sleep more peacefully herself.

"Can you understand that?" she asked Gordon.

Dawn worked for the Ministry of Community and Social Services: assistance to the elderly; elder abuse, old people stuck in their homes; it was a problem the government knew very little about. It was necessary to conduct active research, Dawn explained to Gordon—in-the-home interviews. That was why she was taking his course: Techniques of Social Research. She had also recently become interested in the issue of pay equity, and other political matters. Gordon said little about these interests of hers, because he thought they would soon change again anyway.

Dawn's husband was an alcoholic. She'd left him after five years of marriage, closed years at home with infant children and an apartment in Newmarket, twenty miles north of the city. Now she was reforming her life with a burst of activity—a new career, new interests, new friends, Gordon. Gordon didn't mean to be cynical, but it was a pattern of behaviour he was familiar with. He was a consultant to firms which specialized in selling things to people like Dawn. Things like health club memberships and package tours to Cuba.

Sometimes Gordon would hear Dawn having long, complicated discussions on the telephone with her friend

Wilma, her voice intense and almost cheerful, and he would be glad, for it seemed to him that she was making headway. But when he came into the room, she would hang up.

Perhaps if he had known her longer, if they had been married, or if there had not been children, he would indeed have learned how to help, as the therapist said, and how to talk to Dawn about what had happened.

It was an immense, horrible thing that had happened to her, an outrage, a criminal offense.

It was a small, mean, horrible thing that had happened to him.

Gordon's friends at the squash club had smiled when he first told them about Dawn. Some of them were envious, especially those who were single again. They weren't university professors, and did not have the opportunities that he had to meet women. Gordon had been divorced for four years, but the affairs—dalliances, he called them—had started a couple of years before that. In other matters Gordon was scrupulously honest. He was attentive to his friends. He drank little. From squash and tennis he was in excellent shape for a person of his age.

"When are we going to meet her?" they would ask.

Never. And now they said nothing to him about what had happened. They didn't know Dawn after all, and they didn't know what to say. They didn't think of Gordon's girlfriends in those sorts of circumstances, and it rather threw them.

Dawn seemed to be making a speedy recovery. She was back at work in no time, although sometimes wearing the neck brace. She dropped out of his course. She no longer wanted to go to the university at night. And she told him she could not face the idea of going into the homes of strangers to interview them on behalf of the Ministry of Community and Social Services, which is what his course was supposed to be preparing her for.

Gordon had given Dawn the address book, put it in her stocking at Christmas. It was made of blue leather. After Dawn's mother and sister had gone home, and the children were having their naps, he and Dawn had spent Christmas afternoon going through the old address book, carefully transcribing names, addresses and numbers into the new one. Then they had made love.

Gordon had to tell the police officers all about the address book, sitting in bed writing new names in it on a snowy Christmas afternoon. The investigating team consisted of two officers: a man and a woman. This was a recent change in police department procedure. These two officers would follow the investigation right through from beginning to end, so that Dawn would be spared the need of telling the details over and over again to different people. That, too, was a recent change in procedure.

Gordon got the news that night at his office, less than two hours after it happened. Someone had seen Dawn wandering behind the library and had called campus security. They took her straight to the hospital. The first thing the hospital told him was that she had whiplash, that she would be in a brace for a few weeks. Gordon had been playing squash, and had returned to the office to check for messages, to pick up notes to review for the next day's class. The red light on his machine was winking in the dark. There were also messages in his pigeon hole, left there by colleagues who had answered the faculty line during the evening. There were messages on his machine at home too. Gordon was surprised at how they had all tried so hard to get in touch with him, at how established he had become in Dawn's life. There were messages from Wilma, the friend she worked out with; from Kelly and Morgan's baby sitter, from Mrs. Russell who lived downstairs from Dawn, from the hospital, and from Dawn's mother.

Dawn had been raised by her mother in the country, near the town of Bradford. "Potato country," she told him. In recent years, Gordon had found himself more attracted to the women in his extension classes than to his regular students. They were older than the full-time students who were in his day classes. They were usually less educated. They were often from out of town. If Gordon had been asked to think about the matter professionally, as a marketing consultant, he might have classified many of them as "emulators"—people trying to enter the mainstream, to move up one or two social strata. Such people were increasingly recognized as a distinct market segment.

One time, when she was telling Gordon something about her youth (he had been only half listening, reading a book about social typologies) she said, "We used to go to the plaza."

"What, in New York?"

She had meant the local shopping plaza. It was a great joke for him, an affectionate joke. Dawn had never heard of the Plaza Hotel in New York City, which Gordon found amazing.

Gordon had been to the house near Bradford only once, at Thanksgiving, near the beginning, when she was eager that her sister and mother meet him. After that he had shown such reluctance that they had never gone there again.

Her father was long gone. One of his friends said, "You always get involved with these women without fathers. If they'd had fathers, they wouldn't want to go screwing around with an old fart like you."

Dawn was a "mature student." She was twenty-six. Gordon was forty-three.

The woman police officer gave Gordon a medical lab requisition form, and asked him to take it either to his own doctor or to a lab. Did they suspect him of anything? No, she'd told him. It was a question of ruling things out. Was he absolutely required to have the blood test? They had simply thought he would want to help. Gordon did not like this at all. From his conversation with the police officer, he understood that she knew when he and Dawn had last had sexual intercourse. What kinds of other details about him did they know? What had she told them about him?

It was the hospital who had brought the police into the matter. They were obliged to do so. Dawn told Gordon that she would never have gone to the police on her own. Later, in the spring, she changed her mind about this. She told him that she would have eventually gone to the police on her own, and that if he was annoyed, he ought to be annoyed at her, not at the police or the hospital or Wilma or the Crisis Centre.

Gordon didn't like it, he thought of it as stirring things up. He went to a lab downtown rather than to his own doctor or to the university clinic. The lab results went straight to the police and he heard nothing more about them.

One day over a rather awkward lunch (their conversation was becoming as stilted as their love making) she said that the therapist to whom she had been referred by the Crisis Centre wanted to speak to him. Gordon answered her in a monosyllable. They were sitting kitty-corner in the restaurant and he did not turn to face her. He knew that everything in his body language was sending the wrong message. He knew it was irrational, but he felt an instinctual resistance to visiting a counselor.

Dawn developed some kind of skin infection, a direct result of the attack, as it turned out. She awoke Gordon on a Saturday morning, the first morning he had spent the whole night at her apartment since it had happened. She awoke him with her shrieks, called him into the bathroom.

Then she wouldn't let him look. "Get out of here," she yelled, "get out of my bathroom. Get out of the house." Gordon had gone straight to his own doctor. Naturally he was worried that he might be infected. He was also worried that he might have been the one who had infected her. He was not thinking rationally.

After this, Gordon decided to see the therapist at the Crisis Centre in spite of his reservations. He wanted to be supportive. And he learned all sorts of things: that an attack like the one against Dawn occurs once every six minutes; that it is an act of violence, not of passion; that it is part of a whole web of attitudes. Look at the advertisements for lingerie and work-out clubs in the bus shelters. Gordon did not know how he was supposed to react to these particular observations.

He stopped going to the squash club as much as he used to. He no longer liked the atmosphere there. He had lost his taste for the banter.

Dawn was furious. Her rage consumed her like a fire, and it frightened Gordon. She said that people like the man who had attacked her should be castrated. She said it often. "It's good to talk about it," Gordon told her, but he wondered how long this would go on.

The smell of cigarette smoke was in Dawn's hair and clothes all the time now. When she ran out of cigarettes she would sometimes call him. Could he stop at Becker's on the way over and pick up a pack?

She had always smoked, but never like this. She used to stop for perhaps two weeks, then take it up again. Once she had stopped for almost three weeks. Then she started again, saying she would quit when she wanted to, not to please anybody else, and that she wasn't ready yet. When Gordon thought about it now, he told himself that, apart from anything else, her smoking would have become an issue someday. He told himself that it alone would have doomed them. How he hated the smell.

The assailant was never caught.

Spring came. The campus turned brown as the snow thawed and ran down the sidewalks in gritty rivulets. Gordon became busier with exams and marking papers. In past years, this was when his dalliances had naturally ended. Not this year. Gordon wondered about the future. Like Dawn, he started to replay the events of that night in his head over and over and over again.

She has just left the library. It is a suddenly warm night with a balmy breeze, exhilarating for early February. The street is quiet, the pavement slick and black. She sees a man come running from the darkness on the other side of the road. She sees him quite clearly. He seems to be running towards the bus stop. She wonders: Why is he running when the bus is nowhere in sight? Is he being chased? She feels the first prickling of alarm. He grabs her around the neck as he runs by; it feels as though she has been hit by a car. She begins to fall, but the man stops her, drags her by her shoulder and hair and upper arm. He pulls her across the wet snow and grass to one of the deep sloped window wells behind the library. He holds what she believes to be a kitchen knife to her throat....

At the hospital, the mark of the knife was determined to be seven centimetres below Dawn's left ear.

One late afternoon during a spring thunderstorm, two months after she had been raped, Dawn phoned Gordon at his office, insisting to the secretary that she needed him, that he must come to the phone.

"Yes," Gordon said. He was irritated, he couldn't help it. He was half-way through his graduate seminar. The secretary had to leave the phones unattended and walk down the hall to get him, since there were, of course, no phones in the seminar rooms. "What is it?"

"It's the children." She was gasping, terrified. She seemed barely able to speak.

Kelly and Morgan were supposed to be at home, they were to have been dropped off by the sitter at five o'clock. Another babysitter had been arranged for evening—the usual Thursday routine. But there was no answer at the apartment. There was no answer at the sitter's. The day care and the school were closed. She could not get through to Mrs. Russell downstairs. She was delayed in the far northwest of the city. She was thinking about the address book, missing since the night of the attack, and the details that were written there.

Gordon left the university in the middle of his graduate seminar and drove his black BMW across town, through the rain. He took side streets, avoiding the up-town rush-hour traffic. He parked in front of a neighbour's house, blocking the drive. He ran up the stairs, stumbling in his haste. His heart was racing. The house was in darkness. He knocked on the door. No answer. He began to call, "Morgan? Morgan are you in there? Kelly?" Droplets of water flew from his raincoat as he pounded the door.

"Gordon?" A child's voice.

Gordon turned in response, shielding his eyes from the light. Morgan stood at the landing holding a flashlight. "Gordon, guess what? The lights went out! We had to go out and buy a flashlight!" The boy shifted the light, and now Gordon could see Morgan, Kelly, and Tracey, the sitter. Mrs. Russell stood behind them, outlined in the doorway of her apartment by candlelight.

Gordon was by the children in an instant, burying his head in their hair, hugging so hard that he almost hurt them. There were tears in his eyes.

Around this time Dawn started asking Gordon a certain type of question, which he found pointed and aggressive. Was he in the habit of having affairs with his students? What did he think of older men having relationships with younger women? "I mean, where it becomes a pattern." She asked him if there was a name for that sort of thing. Was it a recognized psychographic type?

Gordon began to think that the weight of these things on a love affair like theirs was simply too much—the address book, the venereal infection, the police, the blood tests, the sexual difficulties that had arisen, now these questions. He felt exhausted.

"I notice we never go to your house," Dawn said. "I have never met your parents. I notice you keep much of your life private."

"Do you ever wonder about what you do? I mean, did you really go to Stanford, do psychology, so you could help hustle panty hose to working women?" she asked

Good point.

Like a priest in middle-age, Gordon had become plagued by doubts. He had gone to graduate school despite the misgivings of his parents. His father was a lawyer, his mother's family owned a small steel company. Gordon had continued with his studies not out of a love of scholarship but because he would do more with his life than enter the steel business or become a solicitor. But even while he was still in graduate school, he came to see his decision as little more than an elaborate gesture. Then he found a branch of his discipline that was closely allied with the needs of the marketplace. He busied himself with his private consulting practice. He took a cross-appointment to the business school. He began to teach extension classes and summer school, to students who were in the real world, as people said at the university.

"I do my best," he answered.

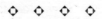

Someone with whom Gordon played tennis, a professor of modern literature, showed him the article. It appeared in a

small quarterly, edited by a collective. He recognized the name of one of members of the collective as Dawn's friend Wilma. The details were precise—the blue leather notebook with the fine-lined pages at the back, the deterioration of their love making. And besides the details, certain themes, parallels between the crime and the older man/younger woman and student/teacher relationships. Something about the ads in bus shelters. The opening lines read: "Last fall I had an affair with my professor. I was also raped. I never found out the identity of the rapist."

He telephoned her, enraged. It was absolutely unfair.

It was nothing personal, she told him. She had been advised to write about it by the therapist—a kind of exorcism.

And she added, "I've given up smoking. I couldn't have done it without the help of the group."

Five o'clock, a Thursday afternoon. The final meeting of Gordon's graduate seminar. The seminar leader for that day has given the summary of her paper, which all the students are supposed to have read, and they are ready to move on to the questions and discussion. There is one of those momentary silences, when the afternoon holds its breath. The fidgeting stops. They look up from the table, from their books and papers. They look at Gordon. He is perfectly still, head tilted, eyes towards the door. He is waiting, listening in that perfect silence for the foot steps of the faculty secretary coming down the hall to interrupt the seminar, to tell him that he is needed, that he must come to the phone at once.

GOOD HANDS

✧　✧　✧　✧

Tillman Grady waited on a leatherette couch outside Courtroom Five, as ordered. He had the letter from his ex, Louise, crumpled in the right rear pocket of his pants, the dark blue golf pants she'd bought him four years ago on a post-season holiday to Florida. Now, together with Louise and her lawyer, Grady was about to perpetrate fraud on the Ministry of Community and Social Services, the provincial government, the powers that be. That was something, anyway.

He reached into his pocket for the switchblade he often carried, the guys on the team called it his worry beads, but thought the better of it. He was in a court house, after all.

Where was Louise, anyway? He took out the letter. "I know you have no obligation to me now, Tillman, and certainly not to Del," she had written. "I only ask for the sake of the little girl. From your own past, Tillman, you, of all people, must know the damage that can transpire in foster homes...."

Transpire? Jesus H. Christ. Was she trying to put him down? Maybe the lawyer had told her what to say. She was the one who had instructed them both to appear April 16, at two o'clock at the court, Provincial Division, 311 Jarvis Street.

Only in the last sentence did Louise sound like herself. "Don't screw up this time, Grady," she wrote in her big perfect slanting letters, the way they had been taught in high school. Now Louise taught that course herself, only they called it Business Economics, and computing had replaced penmanship. Who were they trying to fool? Business Economics was the girls' equivalent of Shop; it was for people who weren't supposed to be headed for university.

Grady slouched in the chair, his legs sprawled out in front of him on the tile floor. The chairs in the waiting area weren't designed for people like him: six foot four, close to three hundred pounds. In his playing days—his 'professional days' he called them, although he still played a little Senior B, just in case—he had weighed in at around two twenty.

He leaned back, his head against the metal railing of the stairwell. He closed his eyes. For weeks he had been having this day dream. He's on his skates, circling at the blue line, waiting for something to happen, waiting for the pass, never tiring. But lately it was becoming harder to capture, the idea that they would call him up again. A picture he could not make whole.

An attendant came through the waiting area and opened the window. It was an unseasonably hot day, the beginning of spring. Grady had arrived at the court house early because it was hard to gauge how long the drive from Barrie would take. Dutch had driven him; Grady was under a six month suspension for drunk driving.

For the second time since he'd arrived, he strolled the two

flights of stairs to the basement men's room for a cigarette. When he came back up, he saw that Louise and Martha had arrived. Louise was sitting in the next waiting area. She held the baby, now a year old, in her arms. Grady had not been expecting that. It stopped him dead. Martha was standing sentinel, scanning the lobby. As soon as she saw Grady on the stairs, she walked quickly over to him. She was a tall woman with dark hair and large features.

"There's been a delay Tillman, family court judge ran late this morning. We've got about a half hour wait."

She stood at the top of the stairs staring at him. She wore a blue jacket and skirt, dark mesh stockings, high black heels. She told him she didn't want him to speak to Louise before the court appearance.

He shrugged his shoulders. He said, "Christ. I can't just come down here at the drop of a hat, you know." He turned and headed back down to the lower lobby entrance.

"Grady," Martha called after him. "Half an hour. Don't go far."

"Bitch," he said, under his breath.

He was angry, not so much at Martha as at the whole god-damn situation. And the sad truth was, he could easily drop everything and drive down to Toronto at the drop of a hat, and Martha knew it.

When he'd returned to Barrie after his two years with the pros—when it became crystal clear even to him they weren't going to be calling him again—the dairy gave him a raise, a new title, and less work: Manager, Special Events and Promotions. All he had to do was show up and talk to people once in a while. About the Leafs. About the players he'd known. He did Rotary Clubs and school assemblies and church halls and the opening of strip malls. He talked about good sportsmanship and the importance of drinking milk. He told kids how vital it was to stay in school, how sixteen percent of adults couldn't read simple instructions. It used to make Louise roll her eyes.

Tillman Grady had driven a dairy truck from the time he was sixteen until he was twenty-three, the year was invited to the Leaf camp for tryouts. It made a splash in the papers. Usually if you weren't picked up by the time you were eighteen, you were through, especially with the Europeans and U.S. college players coming along. But a member of the Toronto scouting staff, a part-timer, a man he'd known in high school, spotted Grady on one on his road trips through central Ontario. The Dutchman. He was about fifty then. He called Grady over after the first period at a game in Collingwood. "Hey Grady, you been working on that shot? Where'd you get those hands?"

In the second period, Grady delivered a couple of checks that shook the boards. He was big. The Dutchman was impressed.

Still, it was a long shot. The trouble with Tillman Grady, the book on Tillman Grady ("There's a book on everyone, you know that, eh, Grady? Just like the ponies") was that he couldn't skate. "Plus you got to cut back on your drinking." That's what O'Brien, the General Manager, had said.

O'Brien sent him to a power skating clinic the first year he was with the team. But how could you teach a twenty-four year old to skate? You couldn't. Grady knew his skating looked heavy, as though he were pushing something, and that he stood straight up when he skated. Delbert, his buddy, who'd come up right out of Junior A, said, "It's about your skating Grady—you don't bend. You skate standing straight up. You gotta pump, you know? Christ, you look like a lamp post coming down the rink—worse than Glennie, worse than Mckenny."

At the power-skating camp, they told him, "It's like skiing, or starting a foot race. If you don't have your weight low, don't have your legs bent, you have nothing to push against."

They tried him at centre. He would be like Esposito, a thug loitering in front of the net, with his good hands and his stick on the ice, waiting for something to happen. But Esposito could move it when he wanted to. Grady couldn't. They put him back on defense. One not bad season; one fair season. Then there was the back injury. That was two years ago. They never got back to him after that.

Grady walked down the steps of the court house and crossed Jarvis Street to the restaurant where the Dutchman was waiting for him.

"You through already?" Dutch asked him.

"Haven't even started." Grady ordered two beers.

Couldn't skate but he had good hands. At camp, they were always telling them. "Don't hold it hard, like you're hanging on for dear life. Hold it soft." But Grady had never needed those lessons. He knew it instinctively. He held a hockey stick in his hands as though it were something delicate, an injured bird. Something deft and perfect. The way he handled that switchblade.

"You better put that damn thing away," said Dutch. "The waitress is starting to stare. This ain't the Dominion Hotel, you know. Why'd you bring the knife with you, anyway?"

"Thought I might stab Del," said Grady.

"Oh, brilliant," said Dutch. "Stab Del, one of your best buddies, the guy who showed you how to drop a pass. Stab him on the steps of the court house—brilliant idea. The guy who looked after your wife when you took off."

"Looked after her? Fucking looked after her, alright."

"Excuse me? Weren't you off looking after someone yourself. And the person you picked—most boneheaded move I ever heard of."

It was probably his hands that had captivated Louise in the first place, that's what Grady thought. She noticed those things because of her job; she touched your hands, guided you, when she was showing you how to write.

Management had brought her in to give the dairy drivers a two-day course in penmanship and handwriting because they were getting so many orders wrong, getting so many complaints from restaurants and supermarkets and corner stores and even the homes they still delivered to. Louise had started the course with a little lecture that made a lot of the guys squirm in their seats.

"The reading and writing skills of sixteen percent of Canadian adults are too poor to allow them to deal with most of the written material used in everyday life." You could tell it was a lecture she'd given before.

"That's what we are," said some goofball in the back row. "A bunch of sixteen percenters."

Louise smiled down at them. "Don't worry. Just because you have poor reading and writing skills doesn't mean you're less intelligent then everyone else. That's a myth."

Louise had beaten the odds. She'd graduated from the Special Commercial stream and gone to university and teacher's college. She was the only person Grady knew who had two degrees. She'd lightly held his wrist and fingers, trying to show him how to make his letters. She'd brought him up to the front of the class to write his vowels on the blackboard. ("Hey Grady, show us how you do your slap shot! Show us how you hold your shaft!") She'd asked him out for coffee at the end of the second day. And he had told her then his great news, his miracle, that he'd been asked to the Leaf camp.

When she found out he was a hockey player, it seemed to speed things up. She asked him home to meet her dad and her brothers. He helped them with the haying that August, instead of going on a honeymoon. "You just want to work on your body," she'd kidded him. "Like Bobby Hull."

Ten months later, after his first season in the NHL, they finally took that honeymoon to Florida.

"The clock is ticking," Louise said. She was thirty years old, almost five years older than Grady, and she wanted to have children, had been hoping to ever since they'd been married. When they got back from Florida, they began the endless round of tests.

Grady learned to skate on a pond near his house. Later he and his friends would walk across the fields to Kempenfelt Bay, their sticks and skates dangling over their shoulders. Sometimes, after a couple of warm days with no snow, then a cold snap, the Bay would be smooth white ice as far as the eye could see. You could skate like the wind. Towards the end of the season, cracks would start to appear. It would stop you dead in your tracks: the *thwack* of splitting ice reverberating across the bay like a gunshot.

One early spring, Grady was maybe fourteen years old, he and Del were walking along the edge of the bay with King, Del's old black Lab. The wind was warm and sweet. Suddenly King turned, he'd caught a whiff of something, and took off across the ice. A few seconds later they heard the crack.

"King, come back here! Come back!"

The dog turned, tail wagging, waiting. His rear legs fell though the ice. He scrambled at the ice with his front paws, yelping. Del tried to walk out, but the ice began to shift and sway. King slid further into the black water.

The whole time Del was yelling. "Oh, Jesus Christ, Jesus Christ! Come on King, come on boy."

Grady watched in silence. There was nothing he could do. The dog was gone in about five minutes. Del stopped yelling. There was only the sound of water stirring and gurgling along the shore.

That was what Louise's news was like, after her visit to the hospital in Toronto. "I can't have children." A crack in the ice that reverberated through every moment of their lives.

❖ ❖ ❖ ❖

"What's wrong, Grady?" said Dutch. "You hardly said a word since you come in here."

"Louise brought the little one. The baby, Trudy Diane. She has her with her in the court over there."

"So, what'd you expect? Isn't that what this whole scam's all about?"

Grady signalled for another beer.

"I think you better have a coffee," said Dutch. "You don't want to go in there farting and burping, the happy father. Another thing, you know any tall women with purple lipstick? Looks Jewish, if I may be allowed to say so."

"Why?" said Grady.

"'Cause she's sitting over there watching you like a hawk. Don't look."

But Grady did look. "Jesus H. Christ."

"An old fan?" said Dutch.

"The goddamn social worker, the one who did the home study, the one who found the baby in the first place. She's gonna wonder why I'm not with Louise."

"Take it easy, you're allowed to have a drink with the old Dutchman. You're supposed to be celebrating, after all."

Dutch leaned forward, grinned broadly, and raised his glass to the social worker.

"What I can't understand," said Dutch, "is how you got that lawyer to go along with it."

"Had nothing to do with me. Martha's a friend of Louise's. Says the government shouldn't be telling women they can't have kids without a man in the first place."

"Pardon me for living," said Dutch.

When Louise had told him about the plan, he'd been amazed. He'd never been that big on adoption in the first place, even after the waiting. "You mean, you still want to go ahead with this thing?"

"You're goddamn right I'm going ahead. I don't give a

sweet goddamn about you and your little girlfriend. I'm keeping this baby if I have to skip the country."

"How come you had to get mixed up with Del, anyway?" he'd asked her, a little forlorn.

"Grady, you asshole. I can't believe you're saying this. You take incredible advantage, take some...confused girl to a motel room, and you ask me about Del. I'll tell you about Del. He's been a real help. Someone I can count on, which is a hell of a lot more than anyone can say for you. Anything I do with Del, that's none of your fucking business."

The waitress brought the coffee.

"Dutch, you think they might call me up again some time?" Grady said. "Jesus, that'd show 'em."

"It ain't going to happen," said Dutch. "You had your shot. Luckier than most."

The social worker stood up, picked up her briefcase and strode by them with barely a nod.

"She doesn't like it," Grady said. "Me sitting here drinking with you, Dutch. Maybe she suspects something." He looked at his watch. What if he'd screwed the whole thing up? He grabbed Dutch's arm. "Dutch, you've got to come over there with me."

They were late. When they opened the doors to Court Room Five, the others were already gathered at the front. The social worker and Louise, the baby beside in her a carry-chair, were already seated. Martha and Del were standing, clearly waiting for Grady. There was no one else in the room but the judge at the bench and a clerk. The judge appeared to be going through some papers.

"Jesus," said Dutch. "The judge is a lady too. Aren't there

42

any men left?"

Martha came down the aisle towards them. "Who's this?" she asked Grady.

"Friend of the family," said Dutch.

Martha took Grady by the arm. "You have to sit next to Louise," she said.

As he waited for them to shuffle along the bench (Louise had to pick up the carry-chair, the social worker had to rearrange her papers), Grady found himself standing beside Del.

"Hello Grady."

"Del."

Grady looked down at the baby and it struck him that they were talking about a whole life here, a new life, someone's future. He felt weak in the knees. The urge to stab Del had gone.

"I was always sorry about that dog," Grady said.

"What?" Del said.

"King, that time he fell through the ice. I should've said something. I don't know."

"Yeah, well."

They took their seats. Grady didn't look at Louise but he could tell she was nervous. "How long will this take?" Louise asked Martha.

Then the Judge and the machinery of the Court took over. There was a few questions for Martha about documents from the Ministry, about how the father was not aware that a child had been born. Stuff about the home study, the various deadlines and regulations that had been met. Grady was in a daze, staring at the flag, the picture of the Queen. Suddenly the judge was looking at him, smiling. For some reason she had just announced the date.

"As a judge, this is among the nicest responsibilities I have to perform. That's why I always save them until last. I hereby sign the Adoption Order in respect of Trudy Diane Grady. Congratulations, Tillman and Louise. Do the new parents have anything to add?"

"Yes," said Grady. And then, "No, your honour."

"Congratulations."

"I'm out of here," said Dutch. "See you across the road."

The hearing was over. Louise picked up the carry-chair and left by the far aisle. Martha stood to go. Then she turned to Grady. "I just I want to tell you Grady, I personally think it's disgusting what you did."

Louise had known something, of course. She just didn't know who it was, at least not at first. He remembered when he'd first taken Lynn to the motel. Underneath her jeans and blouse she'd worn a white camisole. The room had the stale cigarette and perfume smell that he recognized from being on the road. He'd been with plenty of women in hotel rooms, but never like this.

"What would the social worker say about this?" Grady had said.

Lynn laughed nervously. They were both nervous. The pale afternoon light made the room flat, colourless. Afterwards he said to her, "So who was the father?"

"He was just a kid in my class at school, a guy on the football team."

"You go for athletes."

"Really. Only he was smart. Good-looking, great body. It

was a big party in a field after graduation. Things got out of hand. It was a mistake."

"Is this a mistake?"

"Oh, probably. Definitely."

The social worker had told them it was all going to work out, no problem, but that the birth mother wanted to meet the parents. She didn't want it completely open, she'd bow out after that, but she wanted to be sure. Louise had broken down at the last moment, nerves. She was in a state anyway. "Oh, God, how can I ever take this baby into my heart if I meet the mother. You go alone, Grady. You go meet her."

"Hey! I know you. You used to play for the Leafs. How 'bout an autograph." That was the first thing Lynn ever said to him. She was nineteen, great looking. Grady called her up out of the blue two months after the birth, when Trudy Diane was already sleeping in a crib at the foot of his bed, although it wasn't yet final.

He'd been to the motel with her four times altogether.

Grady sat, exhausted, in the empty court room. Outside, dust swirled along the sidewalks kicking up scraps of paper. Spring. He sat forward, then hurried from the room. The others had already left the lobby. Louise turned when he came through the double glass doors onto the court house steps.

"Hiya Grady," she said. I hear they took your license away again. How'd you get down here."

"The Dutchman drove me."

"Yeah? So say hello to him for me."

She turned to go. Del was down on the sidewalk, waiting by the open door of a taxi. Grady called after her.

"Hey, Louise, I miss you. The little one." He stared at the

baby. "Trudy Diane Grady." It was the first time he'd ever said her full name. "I thought, you know, I might come by some time."

Louise half-turned to face him. There was a ghost of a smile on her lips. "That'd be real nice, Tillman."

THE DREAM KING

◇　◇　◇　◇

The first time it happened was a morning in February when Zimmerman was running for the bus. The sky was clear, the sun just over the horizon: pale yellow and electric blue. The air was cold, so cold it seared his lungs, and Zimmerman did not want to be left waiting on the corner. The cold bothered him now, even on those bright days when the snow sparkled. He shouted. The driver saw him through the rear-view mirror and stopped the bus, part way out into the traffic. Cars honked. Zimmerman ran faster. There was a driveway to cross before he reached the bus stop. He jumped from the curb at the edge of the driveway, to clear a patch of sheet ice, and that was when it happened—a momentary sensation, a fraction of a second. He was airborne, a fluttering bird. Zimmerman's heart raced at the sensation.

Then he landed on the asphalt drive. He was back on the ground, the bus was revving, spewing diesel fumes into the morning air. The bus pulled away as Zimmerman yanked his briefcase through the accordion doors. The driver, who knew Zimmerman by acquaintance, was looking out the side view mirror, gripping the steering wheel. When he turned and saw Zimmerman, pale and sweating in that cold, he said, "Are you all right?"

Zimmerman was breathing hard. "Fine," he said, though his heart still raced.

Zimmerman spent the rest of the day in court, an endless civil case, multinational corporations battling over mineral rights, and he didn't think of it again.

The second incident was a week later at the tennis club, men's doubles. His partner was Bob Newton, the family physician. They were playing under the inflated bubble roof. The light from the high arc lamps reflected from the pale plastic onto the tennis courts in a way that reminded Zimmerman of distant summer evenings. Zimmerman later described this to Anne, how the pale green light was disorienting, as though he were looking for an explanation.

Zimmerman ran back to take a high looping shot after the first bounce. He would have to jump or the ball would hit the wall behind him and go out of play. He jumped and for a fraction of a second he didn't think would return to earth. Time slowed. He reached out to touch the cool latex skin of the bubble with his fingertips and pushed himself back to earth. He turned to see if the others had noticed, but nobody said anything. Bob Newton, only a few feet away, said, "Good shot, but you shouldn't be jumping like that. Not at our age."

Zimmerman was fifty-two. He had a mild case of tennis elbow, tendonitis in his wrist, a bad rotator cuff, slightly raised cholesterol levels (all the usual ailments) and the threat of a bad heart. He'd cut back on fats, given up the few cigars he used to smoke, reduced his drinking. He hardly missed these things any more: his cigars, a drink at lunch now and then, the ability to run down a ground stroke. It occurred to him that he had been giving things up all his life. It was a part of the process of growing old, the diminishing of choice.

When, as a child, Zimmerman had learned of the small blue and green planet, its single moon spinning in space, he had been fascinated and elated. Fascinated by the immenseness of space, elated by the possibilities. He imagined that he might fly away. He and his friends would walk home from school hanging on to lamp posts, the wooden fence, the trunks of the spindly young trees, still swaddled in gauze, that grew in that new neighbourhood where he was raised. This was after the war, and suburban development sprawled every-where, taking over woods and meadows. How was it that the earth, spinning so fast, did not send everyone flying off into space?

"Gravity," said his father. "That's the answer." He didn't look up from his newspaper. "Have you done your homework yet? You want to grow up to be a lawyer, don't you."

No answer.

"Well, *I* want you to grow up to be a lawyer."

"Yes, sir."

It was shortly after this, the end of grade six, that he was sent to boarding school.

❖ ❖ ❖ ❖

At home that evening, Zimmerman told Anne about the incidents at the bus stop and at the tennis club.

"Like those dreams you used to have," she said. She was a teacher at a private school for girls, Special Education for the Gifted. "The ones where you were floating."

Zimmerman nodded. When they were first married, twenty-five years ago, he and Anne had lived in a duplex at the edge of a dangerous part of the city, just ahead of the advancing line of gentrification. There were many robberies. Doors and windows had to be bolted tight. Zimmerman would awaken in the night thinking he heard rustling downstairs. He would hear the garage door banging in the wind and imagine the noise providing cover for an intruder forcing his way through the sun room window. Zimmerman would go down to check, armed with the baseball bat.

He was new at his firm then, and he was expected to put in sixteen-hour days. He hated it. He told his father he wanted to leave the firm.

"Leave the firm? What is it you want to do then?"

Play the piano. But Zimmerman didn't say that. Instead he mentioned some idea he had about working in a foreign country. Or perhaps with the city government, helping the poor.

"Don't be ridiculous," said his father. "This is a family firm. You have responsibilities."

So he stayed. And sometimes, when he heard noises in the middle of the night, he would be too tired to get up. On those nights, he would seem to rise from the bed, half-awake and weightless. He would drift downstairs, bumping against the ceiling, and into the sun room.

He told Anne about it. She told him it was quite common. Astral travel, a trick played by the brain as it stirred from sleep to activity. Perhaps even the route to mystical awareness, to another world.

"Yes, like those dreams," Zimmerman said now. "Except that today, I was awake."

Perhaps he was working too hard, too hard for his age. Perhaps he was not getting enough sleep.

"Go with the flow," Anne advised, smiling.

Zimmerman was not a person that friends would have described as a free spirit. He was fastidious and careful. He had never marched at a political demonstration, never smoked marijuana. Anne was four years younger, and she found these things hard to believe.

"Maybe it just means you're in better condition that you think you are," said Anne. She gently poked him in the ribs. "It shows you're a boy at heart. You certainly don't look fifty-two."

She did not seem sympathetic. She was not taking the problem seriously. He was a specialist in resource law and had been busy for years. Sometimes he felt he had been away too much with his work, that they had not talked enough of possibilities, things they might have done.

"I could retire early," he said. "We could move to a foreign country. Or Collingwood."

Anne turned suddenly, caught off-guard. "Is anything wrong?" she asked.

"No," said Zimmerman. "I suppose not." He collapsed,

exhausted, into his chair.

She handed him his whisky and soda. Then she took his hand and led him into the living room. She wanted his advice on the redecoration she was planning, now that the two children had moved out. Should there be earth colours to replace the aquamarine that they had lived with for fifteen years? Earth colours or aquamarine? Zimmerman couldn't say.

The incidents were sporadic. The sensation seemed to be most intense in the morning and in the evening. Remembering that first time at the bus stop, when the sky had been an incandescent yellow-blue, and the evening at the tennis club under the lamps of the green bubble, he began to associate the experience with a certain quality of light: the light of those summer evenings in the pasture behind the house, his mother calling him home for dinner.

Zimmerman was an early riser. He was usually up before the sun. He would have his breakfast, scanning the morning paper or briefs from his office. Then, on the walk to the bus stop, the sun coming over the horizon, he would have that sensation, that he was on the verge of leaving the earth.

April. When Zimmerman walked to the bus stop, gritty mud stuck to his shoes. Warm breezes blew. He noticed crocuses, lilies-of-the-valley, the first tulip buds. The tips of the maple branches were like tightly furled umbrellas. The dead leaves had turned to mulch and the aroma rose from the earth like musk. Zimmerman could smell the earth with every step, and every step he took seemed to send him skyward. It reminded him of his youth, walking on tiptoes, skipping when he ran, taking half-steps to launch himself into the air.

Zimmerman started to walk more carefully. He feared the floating feeling, feared he might leave this life for good, the life he had made, that had made him. Neighbours who saw him said he looked tired, that he ought to take some time off.

In May he gave up taking the bus. From now on he would drive to the office. He felt safely contained in the car. There was no danger of stepping up and suddenly away. After all, there was his work to attend to, his responsibilities.

He went to see Bob Newton, officially, but without making an appointment. He was whisked into the examining room.

"Philip, this is a surprise," said Dr. Newton. "Is it about your new racquet? Bothering your elbow, I suppose. Do you know, before the days of composites, when we still played with those squishy old wooden Maxplys, there was much less tennis elbow. Our bodies are not made for this new world."

Zimmerman explained that it wasn't the tennis elbow or the tendonitis. It was this feeling of lightness.

"What, you mean light-headed?"

"Not light-headedness," said Zimmerman. "I feel as though I'm weightless. As though I'm barely attached. Unconnected."

It was not a complaint Dr. Newton was familiar with. He asked Zimmerman if he'd been overworking, if he was under stress. The answer to these questions was yes, of course. What could he expect?

Dr. Newton asked Zimmerman about his heart. There

was a history of bad hearts on his mother's side. When Zimmerman turned fifty, he'd had a stress cardiogram; everything had been in order. Zimmerman had no real complaints.

"Then there's not much I can do for you," said Dr. Newton. He recommended Zimmerman try to relax. Without much enthusiasm, he offered valium. Zimmerman declined.

"How are the boys?" asked Dr. Newton, walking Zimmerman to the door. Zimmerman said his sons were fine. They had both graduated from university and were entering law school. It was something that had always been assumed of them. Zimmerman did not say that they were dull fellows, though it often struck him that they were.

"And your father?" said Dr. Newton. "How's he?"

"He still comes into the office," said Zimmerman. He paused, gazing out the open window. A warm breeze carried the smell of lilac into the room "He has been eating lunch at the Toronto Club every day for fifty-five years."

"Amazing," said Dr. Newton."

June 21st, the longest day of the year. Zimmerman worked late, as was his custom. Exhausted, he took the elevator to below street level, to the labyrinth-like underground mall that connected with other shopping concourses, the subway, and the multi-layered parking lot where he left his car. It was after nine o'clock, and the concourse was empty. The only sounds were Zimmerman's footsteps on the terrazzo, gleaming under the fluorescent lighting. Zimmerman came to one of the stairways leading up to the street. He stopped. He felt warm summer air against his face. He climbed slowly up the stairs. He was in a large, empty space at the base of a complex of skyscrapers. In the plaza stood newly planted trees, the trunks bound like mummies.

Zimmerman gripped the wrought iron fence around one of the trees. A pale moon glowed against the darkening sky. The air smelled sweet, so sweet, in the twilight. To the north was the brightest star. Elated, Zimmerman let go. Like a balloon at a child's party he floated up beyond the tops of the spindly trees and into the night, beyond the shadowy towers of the city, toward the dark summer sky and the distant stars.

WHAT ON EARTH

◇　◇　◇　◇

"Down in that cellar every afternoon, the blood of dead animals on the floor, rat droppings—can it be good for him?"

Mrs. DeGroot moved one of the silver candlesticks, so that she could better see Patrick's father through the gloom of the dining room. She rested her elbows on the table and intertwined her fingers, awaiting a reply.

As a rule, Patrick never looked at Mrs. DeGroot unless it was absolutely necessary, but he knew that tonight she wore a pale silk blouse, and that her hair was piled high with jewelled barretts. Her musky perfume mingled with the smell of the fish, making Patrick feel slightly ill.

"Shouldn't he be playing outside?" she said.

Patrick had been seated exactly halfway between Mrs. DeGroot and his father, facing the French doors. It was late April. He saw the trees in the garden as skeletons fading in the dusk. Warm breezes had started to ripple across the lake, but Mrs. DeGroot's house remained shut tight behind storm windows. The only sound was the clink of silver on china— Patrick's father elaborately de-boning his salmon trout.

"I understand someone was murdered in that room," said Mrs. DeGroot.

Finally, Patrick's father put down his knife and fork. He leaned slightly towards Mrs. DeGroot, speaking slowly to make his point. "That is only a *story*." Patrick's cheeks burned. His father continued, "It does no harm. I was in secret clubs myself, when I was a boy." He looked at Patrick, smiling a little.

"I only want what's best for Patrick," said Mrs. DeGroot.

"Of course," said Patrick's father. He picked up his knife and fork. He and Mrs. DeGroot each took a melba toast from the silver basket in the middle of the table and returned to the business of their fish. The way this woman eats, Patrick thought: you could hear her jaws clicking! And *what* she eats. Patrick's father never ate stinky fish when he lived at home.

"Might be good for your little Wilhelm to play with the other boys, join in the club," he said to Mrs. DeGroot. "Eh, Patrick?" Patrick saw clearly that his father's smile was fake.

Patrick didn't answer. He was hoping someone would choke on a bone.

Somewhere else in the house, under the watchful eye of the housekeeper, Willie DeGroot was eating his dinner. His food had been cut into small pieces. Willie was not allowed a knife, in case he lost his temper and hurt himself. Or someone else.

"Order, order, order!" said Patrick. He banged the table with the gavel, a chicken bone which he'd cleaned and varnished himself. "This meeting of the Order of the Sacred Blood Stone is now in session!" Two boys sat on a bench in front of him. "Where's Smitty?"

"Smitty had to play baseball," said Walter, a shy boy with a long face and glasses.

"Baseball?" What about the great mysteries? thought Patrick. He picked up one of the pencils lined up on the table and wrote the names of those present. He knew he was losing people. "Has everybody paid their dues?"

"I forgot mine," said Arnold Burston.

"You're two weeks behind."

"How come we have to pay dues anyway? We never spend the money."

"We're saving up for something big. Like a trip to Toronto to see the mummies in the museum."

"I don't want to go to the museum to see the mummies. We ought to buy some cigarettes. We can smoke them down here."

"We're not going to spend the money on cigarettes. What about Walter's asthma?" said Patrick. "Anyway, my mother would smell the smoke. She has a remarkable nose."

The Order of the Sacred Blood Stone met in the basement of Patrick mother's house, in a room that had once been the coal room. Patrick's mother called it the Blood Room because the cat dragged small animals and birds to kill and eat there. Patrick tells everyone it's called the Blood Room because a boy was murdered there. High in one wall was a black hole, the entrance to a crawl space (the way the cat got in) across which Patrick had hung a sheet.

Patrick stood on the table, reached behind the sheet, and returned the money jar to the crawl space. Back in his chair, he said, "The first order of business is new members. We have to kick Smitty out. He never comes to meetings anymore."

"Know what else?" said Arnold.

"What?"

"Smitty says the Sacred Blood Stone is just an old brick that got washed up in the lake. That's what his father said."

Patrick gazed down at the rounded object on his table. He'd found it by the mouth of the creek. It had one long sharp corner, like a hatchet, or a broad arrowhead. Patrick's theory was that the stone was a sacred relic of the Iroquois, which had doubtless figured prominently in ancient ceremonies. Although it did look sort of like a brick, come to think of it.

"People shouldn't be telling the secrets of the Order," he said.

"Know what else?" said Arnold, "Smitty says the Order of the Sacred Blood Stone is for kids. He went to a party with the Grade Eights last week and kissed a girl. He felt her up."

Patrick rapped the gavel. Since nobody could think of new candidates for membership, he said, "What about asking Willie DeGroot to join?"

"Willie DeGroot?" said Arnold. "We don't want Willie DeGroot. He's stunned."

"But he wants to join. He already knows a lot about the club," said Patrick.

"He's an idiot," said Arnold. "He used to go to a special school—an institute. Those thick glasses? He's cracked. He's nuts."

"He's not cracked. Just different. That's what my Dad says. What do you think, Walter?"

"We better take him," said Walter. "No one else wants to join."

"Mrs. DeGroot is a pretzel-bender," said Arnold.

"What's a pretzel-bender?" asked Walter.

"A lady who plays with a guy's weenie."

"Majority rules," said Patrick, cutting off this line of conversation. He rapped the table twice with the gavel. "We talk to Willie officially next week. The second order of business is Walter's dream."

Walter's glasses glinted in the light from the candle on the table.

"I've been concentrating on my dreams," he said. "Eating cheese before I go to bed, trying to remember my dreams when I get up."

"I haven't had a single dream all week," said Arnold, who prided himself on being a realist.

"I've had lots of dreams," said Walter. "Two nights ago, I had one that was so real, I don't think it was a dream."

"What was it?" Patrick asked.

"I think it really happened."

"What really happened?" said Arnold.

"I floated. Away from my body. I could see myself lying on the bed."

"Yeah?" said Arnold, flashing steel from his braces. "Did you have a boner?"

"I floated out the window and over the house. I could see our street, the other houses. I could see Pinewoods Road and the Eighth Line and the railroad shining in the moonlight."

"What's it like to float?" said Patrick.

"It's like flying. Leaving the earth. You can go anywhere."

"Do you have to come back?" Patrick asked. He noted in the minutes that a decision had been reached to make an attempt at floating at the next meeting.

The thing Patrick noticed most about his mother in the weeks following his father's departure was that she was always cold. She would wear old sweaters, like the ones she used to wear when he was a little boy, and she would stand by the window hugging herself, looking out at the grey lake, as though she were waiting for something. The only sound would be the hum of the pump in the tropical aquarium. On those days, Patrick wished something would happen: a tidal wave coming in from Rochester maybe, or a bomb going off in the attic. That would set the house on fire and wake his mother up—wake them all up.

Other times, she would be on the phone endlessly, talking to her friends, or to his aunts. One time, yakking to his grandmother, she burst into tears, loud, frightening sobs. Another day she would be all smiles—smiles and big plans, how they would go to Bermuda or maybe Sun Valley. (Patrick wanted to go to Death Valley, or to Wawa to see the Indian pictographs, but she didn't seem to hear him.) On those days—the days of the big plans—she would sometimes bake: elaborate cookies with dates and nuts, cakes sprinkled with icing sugar and filled with jam. The next day, she'd be back at the living room window, a cup of coffee cradled in her hands, watching the lake. Her attention was like the beam of the lighthouse scanning the horizon; occasionally, Patrick crossed its path and was momentarily dazzled.

He would have liked to have apologized—but for what?

His father had taken an apartment on Navy Street. He seemed never to be in when Patrick called.

◇   ◇   ◇   ◇

Mrs. DeGroot's yellow brick house, the largest on the Lakeshore Road, was a mile from Patrick's. Patrick had been inside only a few times; he made excuses whenever he could. Yet he wanted to see his father. The invitations presented him with a dilemma. Inside, the house was dark and smelled of lemon wax. Mr. DeGroot, who was some kind of international banker, had moved back to Holland about a year before. He had seemed to Paul to be very old. Mrs. DeGroot was English.

"Yes?" she said in her English accent when she opened the door. She knew perfectly well who Patrick was, but she didn't say hello.

"Hello Mrs. DeGroot. Can Willie come out?"

Mrs. DeGroot looked down her nose at the boys, considering. "Just a minute." Patrick and Arnold stood on the front steps, feeling the cool air of the house wafting towards them.

Willie appeared. He looked surprised. Patrick said that they had to talk to him about something important—maybe they should go out back, where it was more private.

Behind the DeGroot's house, the fields which were once used for grazing horses had gone to seed. Mr. DeGroot had been hoping to develop the land, but the neighbours had managed to stop him. The barn had long since fallen down, but the stones of the foundations remained. In a patch of grass in the middle of these foundations, surrounded by stinging nettles, Patrick and Arnold invited Willie DeGroot to join the Order of the Sacred Blood Stone.

"I thought you had to be twelve to get in." Willie, short, thin, and with a high cowlick, eyed them warily. His skin was pink, as though he were lit from within. And there was something about the eyes, the way they darted behind his glasses....

"We changed the rules," said Patrick. "Now you can join if you're nine."

"Yeah, if you're not too scared," said Arnold.

"I'm not scared. Fatty."

"Better watch who you're calling fatty. Liver-lips. Cry-baby." Arnold gestured with his fist.

"It's okay, Arnold," said Patrick. "Willie didn't mean it." He turned to Willie who had moved part-way behind him. "So, Willie, you want to join?"

"I guess so."

"The initiation fee is five bucks."

"Five bucks? It was only a dollar before."

"It's gone up."

"I don't want to pay five dollars."

"Okay. Forget it," said Arnold. "Don't join. Go back to your cage. You'll never know the secrets. Jew. Crazy boy. Dutchie-Jew-crazy boy."

"I already know your stupid secrets. Your stupid stone." Willie's voice began to rise. Patrick's father had told him never to let Willie get excited. He said Willie was a very emotional boy. Willie turned to Patrick. "I'm going to tell your father."

Arnold lunged, grabbing Willie's wrist.

"You know what'll happen if you talk? Do you know?"

Willie began to wail. "Let me go. Let me go!"

Seizing Willie by the shoulders, Arnold threw him into the nettles. Willie screamed—the high-pitched scream that Patrick hated, the scream that made your ears hurt. Willie scrambled in the nettles, trying to pull himself up. Already Patrick could see red welts forming on his arms and legs, and a deep scarlet gash from one of the stones.

On the way home, Arnold said, "Is your dad really moving in with those creeps?"

It's come to this, thought Patrick: I have to take the bus to Toronto for the day if I want to see my father. I have see him at *work*. Maybe I'll keep going-to Montreal. Or to the cottage, and live by myself in the woods. Then they'll see. He clutched his bus ticket.

Earlier in the week Patrick had dropped in at the apartment on Navy Street. His father had actually been there. So had Mrs. DeGroot. Patrick could smell her. Patrick's father sidled out into the hall, shut the door behind him. Patrick was horrified and ashamed. Had Mrs. DeGroot been pretzel-bending? It turned out to be worse. He could tell by the look in his father's eyes.

"We were just talking about you," his father said. "I think you know why. You'd better not come in now. Come to my office for lunch."

He'd phoned Patrick at home to make the arrangements— late in the afternoon, when his mother was out.

Patrick got off the bus at Wellington Street and walked to

his father's club. The diesel fumes had given him a headache. His father greeted him in the lobby, shaking his hand so hard it hurt; it was how his father judged people. They were both wearing dark grey flannels and blue blazers. "A real little gent," said the old man at the desk.

The place where he and his father peed and washed their hands (you could hardly call it a washroom) was dark panelled wood like the reading room at the public library. Another old man in a white jacket stood in the corner watching, then handed them towels when they were finished. Patrick could hardly wait to get out of there.

Over the olives and celery sticks, Patrick's father began. "How are things at school?"

"Fine."

"At home?"

"Fine."

"How's your mother?"

"Fine." Patrick shrugged his shoulders. "I guess."

"Everything is alright with you? Patrick? Patrick, would you like to answer me?"

"I guess so."

Patrick dreaded what might come next. The Talk. He'd had it from both of them. He doesn't want to hear it. Patrick, your mother and I have something to tell you. When two people can't be happy together....We've tried our best, it's nobody's fault, it's what's best for all of us in the end, I'm sure you're old enough to understand. Nobody's perfect.

But I thought you were.

If The Talk comes today, instead of blubbering or going silent, he would bolt. He'd cased the route to the top of the stairs and he estimated that he could be in the subway in about ninety seconds.

But the gods intervened: two old men in pin-striped suits, friends of his father's, shiny-faced, walked over to their table.

"Ah, this must be the young anthropologist!"

After they had gone, Patrick's father said, "This business with Willie joining your club, Mrs. DeGroot is very upset."

His father must have seen something in Patrick's expression. He added, "So was I." He took a sip of his drink. Patrick gulped down half his tomato juice.

"I appreciate that you asked Willie to join because you were trying to please me."

Was this true? Patrick supposed that it was. If he pleased his father, maybe his father would come back. As simple as that.

"It didn't work out. Alright. Perhaps now you should forget about it for a while. Wait until Willie's a little older. I'll apologize for you."

His father raised his finger, a signal to the waitress.

"By the way, the DeGroots are not Jewish. Not that it would matter if they were." His father unfolded the large napkin with a flourish and placed it on his lap. "Let's consider the matter closed." He glanced at his menu. "Now, what would you like for lunch? How 'bout the steak?"

◇ ◇ ◇ ◇

Dusk. The Blood Room was gloomy. The candle cast still shadows on the brick walls.

"Everybody lie down," said Patrick.

The floor in the centre of the room was covered with

blankets which Patrick had borrowed from the twin beds in the guest room. They arranged the blankets and took their places, their feet towards the old coal window.

"Now what?" said Arnold.

"Just relax," said Walter. "Be quiet. Don't move. Look straight up at the ceiling, at the shadows from the candle." As daylight from the high window faded, the shadows deepened. "Now, close your eyes."

They lay still. After several minutes Walter spoke again. "Imagine your body feels really light, your arms and legs don't weigh a thing. Concentrate. Start with your feet. You start to rise up in the air. You can see yourself lying on the floor."

Patrick could no longer feel the cold floor beneath him, had lost the sensation in his body. How warm it was in the Blood Room. The world was falling away. It was happening. It was as though he were floating, like a feather, into space.

And then a faint breeze across his face. He opened his eyes. The candle flickered. Beyond the wavering light, the room was very black.

And then they heard the voice. "ARNOLD BURSTON," said the voice, "ARNOLD BURSTON, YOU WILL DIE!"

Like a jack-knife opening, Arnold snapped upright. Then a thud, a crash. For an instant Arnold froze, wide-eyed, blood streaming down his face.

He sprang to his feet, wobbled momentarily, then ran out the door, through the furnace room, clattered by old bicycles and clay flower pots, ran through the laundry room, and up the steps. Patrick heard the slamming of the screen door, and felt the stirring of warm air down the stairway.

He reached up, yanked down the sheet from the ceiling.

Willie DeGroot turned and scuttled like a crab in the darkness of the crawl space.

◇   ◇   ◇   ◇

"A right royal mess," Patrick's father said to his mother. "A royal bloody mess. I hope you're happy."

Patrick could hear them from the upstairs den where he was supposed to be watching television. Arnold Burston's parents had phoned; they wanted to get the police involved. They wanted to know what Willie DeGroot was doing hiding in a hole in the ceiling.

"A hole in the ceiling," said Patrick's father. "Why on earth were you letting them play in the crawl space?"

"Letting them?" said Patrick's mother. "I wasn't letting them or not letting them. Where were you?"

Arnold's parents had wanted to know where a boy like Willie got hold of an axe, some kind of Indian hatchet. That was how they had described the Sacred Blood Stone. Arnold Burston had needed twenty-seven stitches to close the wound in his head.

"The DeGroot boy should not have been in this house," said Patrick's mother. "How was I to know?"

"If you'd had the damned grates fixed, he never would have been. And they had some sort of fire down there?"

"A candle. A single scented candle. I said they could use it."

A pause. Patrick heard the cupboard opening. The sound of ice and crystal. He crept along the hall and down the stairs.

"You know this means that the DeGroot boy will have to go back to the institute."

"I am truly sorry about that," said his mother.

They were moving into the living room. Patrick stole down the cellar stairs. Their words became indistinct. A few minutes later he heard them calling him, as if in a dream. Then distant footsteps—his father running upstairs to look in the television room. Patrick felt the floor beneath him, cold through the blanket. He sensed that his mother was standing in the doorway. She would have one arm across her chest, he knew, her hand grasping her throat as though she was cold—chilled to the bone. He heard foot steps again. His father entering the Blood Room. It was the first time they had all been together since Patrick's father moved out.

His father says, "Patrick, what on earth are you doing?"

But he doesn't tell them. Doesn't say anything. He lies on the floor, eyes shut tight, concentrating.

FREE, HAS A WEAPON

✧ ✧ ✧ ✧

Three things happened at once: Toto leapt from the coat cupboard demanding his dinner, the stew boiled over, and Henry called out from the upstairs hall.

"Willa? Willa? Are you there?"

Mrs. Ivy put down the suet knife and wiped her hands on her apron. "Yes, yes—of course I'm here." She was speaking as much to herself as to Toto. "Where on earth does he think I am?" She walked across the kitchen, Toto yipping at her heels. She opened the door to the back stairs and called up, "Yes, I'm here, Henry. I'll be right up."

Henry wanted his dinner. He liked an early dinner on Sundays. She heard him shuffling his walker back to the TV room. Behind her, the spilled stew sizzled and smoked on the element.

"Honestly!" said Mrs. Ivy. She walked carefully to the towel rack where the grease rags hung, gripping the counter as she went. She had only recently recovered from a fall herself, a broken ankle. "Honestly!"

Mrs. Ivy had been gently brought up. "Honestly!" was

70

among the strongest of her expletives. In the large dark house on Bay Street where she had been raised (now a funeral home), her father had read from the Bible every night before dinner. On Sundays, no activities were allowed other than rides to the country to visit aged relatives. *Sunday is a day for visiting shut-ins*. (The gardener always drove on these outings. He was not a Methodist. Presumably the Almighty took a more indulgent view toward non-Methodists who broke the Sabbath rule.) Blasphemy was a sin. As for profanity—the famous four letter words—those were a foreign language.

A few months ago, a salesmen had phoned at dinner time. "Would Mr. Ivy like the carpets cleaned?" he had asked. They had a crew in the neighbourhood. "No," Mrs. Ivy had explained. "No, not today, thank you." She couldn't talk just then, she was preparing dinner. "Thank you, no."

"Fuck you, lady," said the man.

She had seen the word in print once or twice—in books and stories by modern lady novelists, books urged on her by Louise—but it was the first time it had ever been addressed to her. She was seventy-five years old. She phoned Louise and told her about it at once. Louise had laughed.

"Welcome to the Nineties." Then she had said, "Really, Mother, it was partly your own fault. Always hang up on those people right away."

"I was only trying to be polite," said Mrs. Ivy. *You should behave towards the postman exactly as you would towards the King of England*. That was something her own mother had taught her.

There was another vulgar word, a word she hadn't realized she knew until that night, a word that must have been lurking in the darkness, waiting. When she thought about it after-wards, she supposed she must have heard the word from one of the drunks who sometimes loitered in front of the church, or in Gore Park. *Never catch the eye of a drunk*. She never had, but still they muttered when you walked by. Where did these people come from? Somewhere east of Gage Street, she sup-posed. Mrs. Ivy had lived in Hamilton all her born days, and she had never been east of Gage Street.

There were the deranged people, too, who wondered away from the Hospital, the "Brow," and down one of the mountain roads into the quiet leafy streets of the city.

Poor souls.

Mrs. Ivy removed the stew from the element and wiped the stove. She returned to the pieces of fat on the cutting board. She liked the feel of the knife in her hand.

Soldiers training in close combat with bayonets are given the following advice: Come at the enemy from underneath—underhand. This is contrary to the notion that most people have, that a knife should be held above the head. A blow from above has almost even odds of striking a rib and deflecting away. You could end up with a strained wrist or a bad cut. On the other hand, even a weak thrust from below will find its way into the soft flesh of the abdomen. A blow from above is easily deflected with a raised arm. A blow from below is impossible to defend against in this way. And if you come from below, the enemy may not realize you're armed. He may not see the weapon until it's too late.

Henry must have told her this, years ago.

He had won his Military Cross at Ortona, south of Rome, Christmas, 1944. Fighting house-to-house. Mouse-holing, it was called: you blew a hole in the roof and came down on the enemy from above.

Every fall Mrs. Ivy made suet cakes studded with seeds and corn with which to feed the birds through the winter. She had been doing this since she was a girl. "If we feed the birds they will stay with us," her mother had said. And it was true, they did; now the cardinals were in the garden year round, and she'd read recently that even robins were beginning to stay. Mrs. Ivy was a devout reader of the newspaper. It gave her an outside view, and matters on which to comment to Henry and Toto.

She was reading *The Spectator* when the phone rang. It was Louise. She called at least twice a week, without fail on Sunday, and often on Wednesday or Thursday as well.

Louise was in the habit of giving her advice about Henry. "You've got to have your own life," Louise would say. "Get out more. Why don't you join Mrs. Ford's group. Take the bus to Toronto, go to the theatre."

"Who would cook Henry's dinner?"

"Let him get his own dinner for once," said Louise. "It won't kill him."

"It's my job to cook dinner," said Mrs. Ivy.

"Why?"

"Well, after all, he worked all those years. The war. And I

don't mind, honestly. I enjoy cooking."

"Right, he worked all those years," said Louise, like a shot. "Then he retired. When do you get to retire? When do you get to stop?"

"Maria does the cleaning, twice a week she comes now. I only do the bed and the kitchen," said Mrs. Ivy.

"It's a rotten bargain, Mother."

But it was a bargain all the same. And Henry was a good husband. It was inconceivable that he would be unfaithful. When she made this point to Louise, she had to be rather diplomatic. Louise's husband Charles—he refused to be called Charlie—had left, had an affair with one of the juniors at the law firm. Henry would never do a thing like that. Charles helped around the house. But what good was helping with the cooking and the cleaning and changing the diapers if he was going to commit adultery? Mrs. Ivy was amazed that Louise could defend him. Charles was second-rate, that's all there was to it as far as she was concerned; unfortunately, this often put rather a strain on relations.

What was less amazing to Mrs. Ivy was that Louise had taken Charles back, less than a year after they had separated. The junior lawyer had left him shortly after he had left Louise, as generally happens in these circumstances. Even she could have told Louise that. Louise said, "It was a mid-life crisis. He was afraid of death."

Afraid of death? Charles was forty-four years old and in perfect health. What on earth did he have to be afraid of?

When Louise took Charles back, Mrs. Ivy had wanted to say to her, "There, you see how complicated it is?" What she had said instead was, "How are you explaining it to the children?"

"I am telling them that Charles and I have made a choice—that this is what we have decided to do."

Choice? Chose to take Charles back? What kind of a choice was that? Mrs. Ivy did not believe this for a moment. She believed that Louise took Charles back because she was trapped. She wanted to tell Louise that the possibility of choice—even the making of very tiny choices—diminishes as the years pass. Instead she had said, "I see."

There was a pause. Then Louise had said, "At least he's not gay." She had gone on to explain once again how this had happened to one of her friends. She said, "Have you heard from Jonathan lately?"

Jonathan was Mrs. Ivy's second child. He had moved to Vancouver.

Mrs. Ivy had not known there was such a thing as homosexuality until she was middle-aged, and when she found out, the idea quite astonished her. Of course there were ladies who lived together—her own aunt. What family did not have a maiden aunt? And she knew confirmed bachelors, like old Mr. Harris at the end of the street. But did they actually do anything? She could not begin to imagine what went on.

Mrs. Ivy was on excellent terms with Jonathan, but the matter was never discussed. She gathered from Louise that he was living with another man, a freelance designer, of cowboy boots. Incredible. Jonathan was an architect. He was thirty-seven. Rather old to be having a roommate.

"I know I shouldn't say this, dear," Mrs. Ivy said to Louise. "And I know there's supposed to be nothing wrong with it, really, but, well, I don't think you should mention this to your father. You know, about Jonathan."

"I wouldn't. He may be difficult, but he's still my father."

Mrs. Ivy carried the tray with the two dishes of stew upstairs to the library. Henry was watching the TV and reading a book. She put her dinner on a low table in front of the chesterfield. She put Henry's bowl on the table beside his whisky. That was the way Henry liked things done. Just so. It was true, what Louise said: he was difficult. One thing she rather disliked was the way he asked for things. His lunch for example. "I think I'll have some cold beef," or "Willa, I'll have the rarebit on toast." Never, "May I please have some of last night's beef?" or "I love that rarebit you make. Could we have some of that? If it's too much trouble, don't bother—I'll boil an egg."

Henry had never said anything like that. He had never boiled an egg in his life.

Tonight, when he had finished both his stew and his drink, he said, "I think I'll have some of those berries."

"But I asked you before dinner. You said you didn't want any berries."

He turned to look at her, his mouth half open.

"I can't keep going up and down those stairs to get you berries. I'm an old woman!" She was almost shouting. She felt her cheeks burning, feverish. She had not spoken to Henry like this since Jonathan was a boy.

Mrs. Ivy was rinsing the plates when the police came. They rang the front doorbell, then they banged the knocker. She hurried to answer; she did not want Henry to waken. "Masterpiece Theatre" had come on and she knew he would probably be sound asleep. He had trouble sleeping in the early hours of morning. "Masterpiece Theatre" was the only peace he had. Mrs. Ivy too, for that matter.

One of the policemen held a clipboard. The grouchy-looking one.

"Mrs. Ivy, is it?" he asked.

"Yes," said Mrs. Ivy.

"And there's a Mr. Ivy?"

"He's asleep."

"No need to wake him," said the other, a nice young man. "We are advising people to keep their doors locked. A fellow has escaped from the Brow."

"Mind if we check your garage, maybe the potting shed?"

"Go right ahead," said Mrs. Ivy.

"Who has escaped?" she asked. "Is he dangerous?"

"Well, not one of the, you know, regular inmates," he answered.

"Not a lunatic, you mean," said Mrs. Ivy. "That's a relief."

"He's a murderer," said the other policeman, who had returned from the garden. "He was up there for a psychiatric examination."

"The cook from the Connaught Hotel?" said Mrs. Ivy. It was a celebrated case, being tried in front of Judge Morrison. The man had strangled his wife.

"That's the one. He's free. Has a weapon."

"A weapon?"

77

"I'm sure you don't need to worry. Only a garden tool. He won't get far. You just keep your door locked." He turned and looked up the driveway, past the garage. There were rutted lanes behind all those houses, from the days when people had coach houses and back entrances. Now those lanes were thick with weeds and nettles.

As a rule Mrs. Ivy tidied as she cooked and then went over everything again immediately after dinner. She looked at the stew pot with the stains on the sides, at the remaining greasy plates and the bone-handled knives which had to be washed by hand. Henry insisted on using them because they had belonged to his mother.

Never start a job you can't finish.

If a thing's worth doing, it's worth doing well.

She called upstairs. "Henry? Henry?" She would do the strawberries anyway, have some herself with a little cream. She carried the colander of berries from the refrigerator to the sink. In the window she saw her reflection and, beyond, the last of the dead maple leaves. *My seventy-fifth October.* The house where she had been raised was only three blocks away.

She would have liked to travel more. But Henry did not like travel, hadn't since the war. He had promised to take her to Italy but he never had.

"Don't you ever resent it, Mother?" Louise had once asked. Mrs. Ivy had not answered. *If you don't have anything nice to say, don't say anything at all.*

When Willa had first met Henry he was an articling student

and an officer in the reserve. The Royal Hamilton Light Infantry, trained for close combat. There was a photograph of him somewhere, taken on a dry foreign plain. In Sicily, perhaps, the summer of 1943. He was standing in front of a jeep, squinting a little, in the bright Mediterranean sun. The Expeditionary Force had just landed. He was over there fighting for his country, so that people like Charles and his friends might grow up to have their mid-life crises and turn into homosexuals in peace.

How dashing he looked in that photograph; the trim moustache, the curl of the lip—almost insolent.

She smiled. Foolish woman. Foolish woman to be thinking thoughts like that of Henry.

There was an immense crash and clatter at the side door, the door to the sun porch. She thought: the cook from the Connaught Hotel? Was the porch door locked? Mrs. Ivy dropped the colander in the sink and limped into the pantry. She picked up the telephone. The line was dead.

The banging stopped. Mrs. Ivy heard him walk from the wooden porch to the back door. She saw his shadow beyond the dim yellow light.

Mrs. Ivy hobbled through the back hall to the side door; she wanted to make sure it was locked. She looked through the window onto the porch.

"Toto!"

There was no blood, mercifully. The police told her later that the dog had been kicked once in the head, the blow had shattered the skull.

Mrs. Ivy returned through the kitchen. She picked up the suet knife as she walked by the counter. It was smaller than the bread knife but larger than the paring knife, solid, sharp.

The sound of splintering glass.

Mrs. Ivy reached for the door knob. Her hands were red from the pulp of the berries. She flipped up the catch and yanked the door open.

He was large, soft, flabby—rather like Charles, in fact. He looked surprised. His hand, long-fingered and incongruously delicate, still gripped the garden shears with which he had smashed the window. He lurched forward, inches from her. He was dressed in light green pyjamas like doctors wear. His breath was rank. These details Mrs. Ivy took in in an instant.

◊ ◊ ◊ ◊

Physiologically, the signs of rage and fear are virtually the same. The hair stands on end. The eyes open wide. The heart beats faster—more blood for the brain, muscles and heart. The skin goes pale. The muscles tighten—this is noticeable even in the face.

He made a slight movement, as though he would push by her.

There he was: big, soft, shambly, ugly, demanding, stupid, selfish.

Movement upstairs. Henry was awake. He called out.

"Willa?" His voice was weak. He was a poor old man with a bad heart, a bad leg and an enormous fear of death. "Willa? Are you there?"

From somewhere down the lane, a light shone through the shrubbery. No doubt the police.

He raised the garden shears over his head, ready to strike.

The word welled up from the darkness of Mrs. Ivy's brain. "Asshole," she said.

She brought the suet knife up from the folds of her skirt and buried it in his gut.

PEARLS AND
COLOURED STONES

◇　◇　◇　◇

Leaving Dr. Raines' office after her third visit, Carmel asked, "Do people ever go crazy in these situations?" She herself was not crazy. She had been diagnosed as clinically depressed. She felt as though she were living under a thick blanket. It wasn't her fault, and she wanted out.

Dr. Raines looked at the floor and scratched his head. They were standing by the door to the waiting room. Carmel saw that he was reluctant to answer, and she thought perhaps it had been a mistake to ask. Dr. Raines was always asking her veiled questions about suicide: Did she ever imagine she might die? Did she fantasize about being dead, about looking down on her own funeral? But that isn't what she had meant at all. She was thinking more along the lines of cutting off all her hair, withdrawing all her money from the bank, taking the next plane to South America. That sort of thing. A radical reordering of priorities.

"Do they ever go right off the deep end?" she asked.

"I suppose sometimes they do," said Dr. Raines. "But not

people like you and me. We're too smart for that. What we've got to do is get you back to liking yourself. See if we can't get Howard in here."

He took her elbow and gently guided her to the door.

The way Carmel holds the basket in her lap irritates Howard. She grips it tightly, like a child afraid her treasure may be snatched away. To Howard she appears pathetic and incongruous in a car that cost close to sixty thousand dollars. The car smells of rich leather. She has said nothing since they left the house, hasn't answered his question. Finally, without turning to look at him, she says, "Burglars."

Earlier that morning, after a latish breakfast—latish is one of Carmel's words—Howard had loaded the Jaguar. The other car in the garage is a black Porsche. Howard rarely uses the Porsche. He says it doesn't really suit him. He's heard the jokes: a Porsche means you're having an affair. Carmel used to call the car Howard's lollipop. She would wink when she said it.

Carmel had come out of the house about twenty minutes after Howard with Amadeus, the Jack Russell which Howard bought her when Anna went away to school, on a leather lead behind her. She wore slacks and a woollen jacket which they had bought at Bloomingdale's on one of their whirlwind trips to New York. Howard and Carmel take frequent short holidays. Short holidays are more convenient for Howard to arrange between his occasional appearances in court, his meetings with boards of directors and executive committees. His clients are mostly large mining and forestry companies with a proclivity to sue, merge and acquire. Carmel does freelance P.R. work, and her schedule is flexible.

Carmel carried nothing to the car but her handbag and the round red basket which had originally been a child's sewing kit.

"Why on earth are you bringing that?" Howard asked. Carmel hadn't answered.

The weekend away is Howard's idea. He wants something to happen. He wants to put the past behind them, but he doesn't know how to do it, if its even possible.

Carmel says, "I was worried about burglars." Still she doesn't turn to look at him as they speed away from the traffic light.

Howard and Carmel live in a neighbourhood of large houses where there have been several recent burglaries. Windows have been smashed, doors broken, the contents of drawers, cupboards and secret places strewn around. Sometimes there has been wanton destruction—obscenities on the walls, electronic equipment wrecked, defecation on the finest carpets. From the outside it's impossible to guess what mayhem lies within. People say this is life at the end of the 20th Century, but the events are shocking to Howard. In his own life violence has been rare.

Carmel says, "I suppose you still won't go and see Dr. Raines." She turns to look at Howard. He knows that she's gauging his response.

Howard says, "We've been over this before." He keeps his eyes fixed on the road.

One morning the previous June, Carmel came downstairs and told Howard that she would like to visit a psychiatrist. Howard was having his breakfast on the terrace. At great cost, and with much thought by a firm of noted landscape architects, the back garden had been planted with small trees, bushes and shrubs in such a way that no other house was visible from where Howard sat. It was a remarkable achievement in a garden that was mid-town in a city of over two million people. But there had been a price to pay; the flowers had to go. There was not a single flowering plant in that garden.

Howard looked up from his morning paper when Carmel told him about the psychiatrist.

"Lots of people I know are doing it," said Carmel. She was more tentative, then, about the decision to see Dr. Raines.

Howard thought about the hundred or so lawyers in the firm where he worked. He thought about the men at the Racquets Club, people on the charitable and private boards on which he sat. None of them were seeing psychiatrists—not as far as Howard knew.

"Fine," said Howard.

"Will you come too?" Carmel said.

"Why on earth would I want to see a bloody shrink?"

At the dinner parties Howard and Carmel attend, people discuss where they hide their jewellery. One woman keeps her diamonds in the bottom of a salt box. Another puts her jewels in a sock in a toy box, or above the pipes in the furnace room. A more elaborate technique is to sew precious stones into the hem of a heavy curtain. What is amazing is how often these secret places are discovered by cunning burglars.

None of the hiding places would be adequate for large quantities of stones, for really valuable jewellery. Daisy Downs' jewels are kept in a basement vault at a downtown bank. Inherited on her grandmother's side, her jewels have their origins in the Polish royal family. So it is rumoured. When Daisy Downs wears her jewels, she must sign a release form for the insurance company. Howard has always been grateful that Carmel doesn't make comparisons, even in fun, between her rather ordinary jewels and those of Daisy Downs. All the same, he once advised Daisy, speaking as her lawyer rather than as her lover, that she ought not to wear her jewels except to really grand events. To wear such stones was asking for trouble.

Carmel keeps her pearls and precious stones in the open, in the small red basket on the bathroom window sill. The basket also contains hair pins, buttons, beads and costume jewellery, coloured balls of soap and bath oil, sachets of perfumed powders. This weekend, Carmel has decided to take the basket with her. As they continue up the highway, she says to Howard, "I want to go through the basket, to separate the pearls from the fakes and coloured stones."

Howard has been in the habit of giving Carmel pearls on anniversaries and special occasions. "Our pearls." The pearls are additions to the necklace he'd given her years before, to make one large string or perhaps a couple of smaller ones.

Carmel somehow never gets around to taking the pearls to the jeweller to have the job finished. One day, the pearls will be passed on to Anna; that is the plan.

Carmel says, "I want to sort things out."

It's a phrase she uses a lot lately.

Just past Midland, they stop at a restaurant beside a gas station. It's the off-season; they are the only people in the place. Carmel holds the basket in her lap. She had not wanted to leave it in the car with the dog. The restaurant is silent except for the faint twang of country music from a radio in the kitchen.

Howard's knife and fork clatter against the thick dinner plate. He finishes his salad. He says to Carmel, "Aren't you having lunch?"

"I'm not hungry," she says.

She has only ordered coffee. She has not been hungry for days, weeks. Her symptoms are changing and Howard feels he ought to do something. He wants to do something, to atone. He worries that it may be too late.

At first, she had seemed to go into a kind stupor. She slept a lot. In the afternoons, she'd lie on the chesterfield in the rose-coloured living room and listen to the same discs on the CD over and over again. Billy Joel. Barbra Streisand. Music that he had never heard before and that he would come to hate. Once or twice he came home early and found her. She would rise from the chesterfield with deliberate casualness. "I was just resting, listening to some music." It was as though he had caught her at something.

Once Howard awoke in the night and found the place in the bed beside him cold and empty. Carmel was in Anna's room, sitting in darkness. The curtains were open and the room was bathed in pale moonlight, criss-crossed by the skeletal shadows of the maple trees. Posters hung on the walls: the Olympics, track and field stars, a picture of Michael Jackson from Anna's pre-running era. On the mantelpiece (the fireplaces in the house were no longer used) were small porcelain figures from England: Peter Rabbit, Mopsy, Flopsy and Cottontail. The room had the emptiness of a child's room after the child has grown and gone.

Carmel looked up at Howard. "Tell me again," she said. "Why did we send Anna away?"

Anna was at boarding school. In Howard's family, children had always been sent to boarding school. Carmel said, "It would be better for me if Anna were at home. Maybe for both of us." Her voice was flat. It was a discussion they had had before. In two years Anna would be entering college; then she would be gone for good.

Howard took Carmel gently by the hand and led her back to the bedroom. It was as though she were sleep walking, but he knew she was awake because he felt her shivering. He pulled the bedclothes around her, brushing her cheek with the back of his fingers. She stared into the darkness.

The sleeping in the afternoons, the listening to music, the waking up in the middle of the night; all this has stopped. Now there is this activity, the sorting through things, the lack of appetite. As he peruses the lunch check, Howard says, "How can you just stop eating?"

Carmel says, "The fight or flight response."

She's taken to wearing her thick dark hair, now with a touch of grey, pulled away from her face and pinned at the back, like an athlete. Howard would like to ask her about this—it's a style he particularly dislikes—but decides against it.

By the time they turn off onto the dirt road that will take them to Georgian Bay, it's mid-afternoon. Early November, the sky is slate grey. At the landing, the parking lot is empty. This is the season Carmel likes here least—no cars, nor the bustle and hot insistence of summer. Most of the slips and moorings are empty. At one of the corrugated metal storage buildings, a couple of Ojibway men work a tractor with a hydraulic lift, putting boats away for the winter.

Carmel watches Howard speaking to the men, asking one of them to take them out to the island. She watches him, the man she married, the man who takes lessons regularly for his tennis and skiing, who dislikes dogs for their messiness, who keeps a list of the books he has read, who take trips to the wilderness with his friends, carefully planned months in advance, who likes strong martinis but who never has a drink after dinner, who denies himself Nanaimo bars (which he loves above all other food) whose weight has not changed in all the years she has known him.

Yet what had he said? That life is tangled and complicated, that the human heart will not be bound, that passion is not orderly, cannot be denied. So where did the two of them meet? Who arranged their appointments? Who planned ahead to make the hotel room reservations?

Howard waves to her from across the parking lot. The boat is loaded, he has the dog in his arms, they are ready.

The journey takes half an hour. The island is the most westerly of them all and faces the open waters of the lake. When they arrive at the boat house, built high on the shore as protection against winter winds, the boatmen unload the luggage and groceries onto the dock. Howard handles the liquor—the wine, the vermouth, the two bottles of Beefeater. He does not like to be caught short. If there is a scene, she knows that Howard will want it to be irrigated with gin. She carries only her large handbag and the little basket of pearls and stones. The dog has bounded ahead. They can hear him yapping at squirrels.

Carmel follows Howard up the path from the dock. The sound of the outboard dies away. They are enveloped by trees. Carmel can smell the pine and earth. The path opens up as they pass through the glade, the only place on the island where grass grows thick and lush. It brushes against Carmen's ankles. She can feel the autumn air, see the pale sun winking through the fir trees.

Carmel met Howard at a dance in the college cafeteria. They were drinking purple Jesus—grain alcohol mixed with grape juice. After dancing to the Rolling Stones ("The Last Time"), Carmel took Howard by the hand and drew him outside to the covered walkway. She stopped suddenly, turned, drew him to her. Their foreheads bumped, then he relaxed and she was kissing him.

"I've been wanting to do that for ages," she said.

A few nights later, lying on one of the hard pews of the chapel amidst their tangled clothing, she said, "What about the island you told me about. Why don't we go there?" Howard was the first person Carmel had known who had inherited money, had gone to boarding schools, had a summer place that had been in the family for generations.

Her own father was a farmer, an immense man, a pillar of the United Church. Once, after they had been married ten years, her father said to Howard, "What kind of lawyer are you anyway?" They were sitting across from one another at the table in the summer kitchen.

"Corporate and commercial," said Howard.

"You ever go into court?"

"Not if I can help it."

"I need a lawyer. You any good?"

Howard shrugged and smiled. "My father was in law. My grandfather too."

"Is that so?" said Carmel's father. Like Carmel, he had piercing blue eyes. "I always thought Carmel should go in for law. In my opinion, she would make an excellent judge."

He had not hired Howard as his lawyer.

Together Carmel and Howard unpack the groceries. The downstairs of the house is in semi-darkness because the men had been in the process of putting the shutters up when Howard called to say they were coming. It strikes Carmel that this is how these summer houses are for most of the year: dark, shuttered, silent except for the creaking of the wind.

Howard goes upstairs to the bedroom. Carmel follows a few minutes later. She stops on the landing to admire the view, the waves coming in from the northwest. She continues upstairs, past the door of their bedroom to the guest room. She lies down.

An unseasonably warm breeze, from the tail end of summer, wafts through the door from the balcony and across Carmel's face. Howard calls her. She does not answer. She realizes now that this is what she had been expecting. It would be part of Howard's solution—the reason he wanted to come here.

Through the wooden walls, she hears him rise from the bed and pad along the hall. He enters the guest room. Carmel does not move. She lies, eyes open wide, staring at the plain pine boards of the ceiling. Howard comes forward, leans over her, kisses her once, then again. After a few moments she acquiesces and puts her arms around his neck. They do not speak. Twenty-two years ago she had come here for the first time, to this room. They arrived at four in the afternoon; they made love on the grass of the glade along the path before they even reached the house.

They doze. The shadows lengthen in the twilight. The air turns cold: early November on the pre-Cambrian shield. They lie tangled under the musky feather quilt, naked.

Like lovers.

When she was introduced to Daisy Downs at a dinner party,

it was immediately clear to Carmel that Howard had already met her. "I am not a fool," she said afterwards, sounding, she knew, like a wronged woman. Daisy had recently moved from Montreal. She was a widow of forty. She also had a connection to Polish royalty. She was an occasional guest of the Rockefellers at Pontico Hills. Her brother was in the British House of Lords. Luncheons and soirées had been arranged to welcome her.

Carmel had asked, "Where did you first meet her anyway?"

"I sit on a board with her."

"You know how fucking pretentious that sounds? 'I sit on a board with her.' Well good for fucking you."

Howard had not responded to this. He never responded to outbursts. After a time Carmel said, "It will never last."

"Pardon?" said Howard. "What will never last?"

"You fool," said Carmel.

She remembers that Howard had tried to appear chastised; the result had been a grin, as though in the midst of it all he could not help feeling satisfied with himself, and his immense, unruly passions. It seemed to Carmel that instead of remorse, Howard felt like a boy in the lives of these two women, and that it was a role he rather liked. "Some kind of stupid adolescent when we talk about it," she told Dr. Raines, "detachment the rest of the time. And irritation. *He's* irritated!"

"And what are your feelings?" Dr. Raines had asked.

Carmel is wide awake. The wind has come up. The house is beginning to creak, the shutters to rattle. She is thinking about tomorrow. A fresh breeze has come up, as though a new day is about to begin.

Roused by the sound of the waves on the shore and the body of his wife beside him, Howard turns and draws Carmel to him. Carmel at once pushes him over, straddles him, lowers herself onto him. She reaches above her head and unclips her hair, falling about her face as though she were twenty again. Her breasts sway rosy pink above him in the half-darkness. Howard closes his eyes.

Something cold and sharp in his throat. He can't breathe. His mouth is full. He begins to choke. His eyes open. Pearls and coloured stones fall from his mouth—spill and gather in the folds of the sheets behind his head. Carmel continues, over and over; she takes pearls and stones from the sewing basket on the bedside table and jams them into his mouth. Some are now deep in the back of his throat. Howard wants to vomit. He will choke on his vomit and the sharp stones. He can't breathe. He lurches forward but Carmel has her left hand flat on his breastbone. He turns his head. Cultured pearls and pink stones fall from his mouth onto the floor. He hears them clatter and roll beneath the bed. He hears the sound of Carmel's bare feet on the floor as she walks from the room.

AND YOU, DO YOU EVER THINK OF ME?

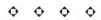

And you, Mr. Singh, in your fine house in New Delhi, overlooking the gardens, the lotus blossoms floating in the pond, or at your flat in Kensington, or at the George V in Paris, do you ever think of me?

Looking up from the bare patch of field where she stood, Estelle Wilson watched a breeze ripple through the hay towards the valley, a yellow wave under the August sun. She touched the sapphires at her neck. She turned toward the house.

◊   ◊   ◊   ◊

On the morning of June 7, a partially mummified body was found in the tall grass of Harold Macnab's front field. The field lay between the highway and the house which Harold shared with Estelle Wilson, his wife of seven years. The field was not used for pasturing because it was so near the highway. It was sparse, noisy, and dirty and this might affect the calving.

The body was found by technicians working on a radio tower on the neighbouring property. They noticed something, which they took to be the body of a calf, lying in the gravel. It had that leathery look, twisted about, like an animal not quite right.

The pathologists in Toronto determined the body to be that of an adult, a small woman.

A small woman? You did not come across so many small women (or men either, for that matter) among the families of Hills County; they tended to be big boned, and they ate well, a lot of potatoes. And, of course, beef, because this was Ontario cattle country.

Possibly the woman was foreign, the police speculated. People began to recall the matter of Anna Ghupta. There were further revelations: the reason the body was well-preserved was not because of the autumn weather; it had been treated by an embalmer, an undertaker.

Someone had dug the body from a graveyard and put it in Harold Macnab's field.

Estelle Wilson watched from the window as William Dixon's blue pickup rattled up the drive toward the house. Dust hung in the air. There was a haze building; it would be a hot day. Estelle felt the first pin-prickling around the eyes. She began to snuffle. She suffered from hay fever, and the morning's medication had not yet taken effect. When she had lived in the city, Estelle had always had air conditioning.

Estelle saw William Dixon climb from the cab of his truck.

She was glad that his son had not come along. Young Willie was a stocky man of twenty-one with short hair and pale eyes that fixed on you unblinking; he made Estelle uncomfortable.

William Dixon and Harold Macnab had been in public school together, forty years before, the same school Estelle visited as part of her job. Except for the city people with their story-book farms, it seemed to Estelle that everyone in Hills County was either related or had known each other since childhood. She was a foreigner here.

When she first came to the County, she would leave her apartment above the hardware store, and drive out to the country to take long walks along gravel roads where the split rail and stump fences of the pioneers grew greyer and more overgrown each year. The fields were a patchwork of dun and green separated by rows of dead elms. There were dips in the land, with ponds and stands of birch and aspen, and when you came out of those valleys, perhaps a sudden view of the Escarpment curling away to distant hills, or a row of poplars shining in the morning sun like obelisks of fire on a Tuscan hillside. It was not the view you expected in Ontario farm country; it was disorienting, and it momentarily took your breath away. Estelle did not like that kind of surprise.

"Estelle," Harold called. "William and I will be going out to see the cattle now. Perhaps you and Hildy will make coffee?" Like many rural people, Harold was rather formal in his speech. He never used profane language, and he spoke quietly—such a contrast to the cacophony of Estelle's first marriage.

Estelle heard Hildy banging the pots as she looked for the coffee maker. She called down the stairs, "Hildy, there's no need for that racket!"

Hildy helped at the farm, in return for a room above the garage, meals, and a little spending money. She was nineteen years old. She had had sex with most of the boys in the area. She had been pregnant three times and delivered once (the child was put up for adoption by the Children's Aid), and now there was the fear of sexually transmitted diseases, STD's the school board called them. There were many policy directives on the matter.

Estelle had never had an STD. She had never been pregnant and, at age forty-six, did not expect to be. Some (among Harold's family especially) wondered how this could be. One elderly woman went so far as to remark, "Having a child made me feel like a real woman." Estelle was glad to have all that behind her. For the first time in her life she was beginning to feel settled.

And yet, there were things that sometimes disturbed her: pictures of foreign cities, certain novels, the way Hildy dressed. Estelle had always known there was a world hidden from hers, a world of people who were not respectable, who lived like animals, who drank whisky and beer and fought in public places. Her friend, Hannah, a social worker with the Board, told Estelle that people on welfare had more sex than other people, and in different ways. "They do it in the middle of the morning. They have nothing else to do," she said. And Estelle knew it was not only poor people; there were women who wore furs next to their skin, who travelled abroad by themselves, who became men's mistresses. This knowledge sometimes preyed on her.

Estelle came down the stairs as Hildy finished cleaning up the breakfast things with a maximum of clatter.

"They say it's devil worshippers," said Hildy.

"Nonsense," said Estelle.

"They eat babies. They chop them up and eat them. They dress up in black robes, like Halloween, like, and kill people for the devil. At midnight. They use garlic."

"And salt and pepper too, I suppose," said Estelle.

Estelle's laughter was a little forced. It was not the satanic rituals business, which she didn't for a moment believe. She knew the strongest religious organization in the community was the Women's Institute. It was not that the body was found on Harold's land—although that was something. It was William Dixon, here for urgent discussion, and a walk to the barn to see the calves when William Dixon was not interested in cows. He had given up farming years ago in favour of ploughing roads for the County.

One time Estelle asked Harold, "How long before I am accepted here, as one of the community?"

"Twenty-five years," said Harold.

Which was sooner than Anna Ghupta. She would never have been accepted.

Estelle saw Harold lean against the door of William Dixon's truck, his checked shirt flapping in the breeze. He was an elder in the church and in the community. He was fifty-eight years old. People looked up to him, sought his advice. Yet when she saw them quietly talking, these country people, she sometimes had the feeling that she was the one who was just stopping by.

When Harold came in, he was more serious than usual. "I must visit Solicitor Howe," he said. That is how they referred to the lawyer in town, as though he were a public official, like the mayor or a county court judge. When the Conservatives had last formed the provincial government, Solicitor Howe had been a member of the legislature, and he was presumed still to have influence. Estelle never got used to his title. Her own family had its share of country solicitors; she thought of them as little more than clerks.

"There may be implications," Harold said.

"Is it do with William Dixon's son, those other boys?" asked Estelle, too quickly.

Harold told her that they were worried about the matter getting into the papers before the ploughing competition, an annual event which brought thousands of dollars into the local economy. Perhaps Solicitor Howe could bring weight to bear to prevent bad publicity. "And there's some kind of foreign gentlemen coming to town," said Harold.

"Foreign gentleman?"

"From India. A Hindoo," he said, exaggerating.

This turned out to be wrong. The man was a Sikh. He arrived in a white Cadillac with smoked windows and took a room at The Highwayman Motor Lodge at the edge of town. Estelle first saw him three days later in front of the Shure-Grain store on Manitoba Street. He wore faultless white trousers, a double-breasted blue blazer with silver buttons, and a deep blue turban.

Until 1981, East Indians were not seen in this part of the country. But as opportunities closer to the city diminished, some began to move farther afield, to the dusty grid, the concessions and side roads laid out by the Imperial bureaucracy more that a century before. Many of the abandoned gas stations along the highway had been reopened by Indian families as variety stores, video rentals, coffee and donut shops, even an Indian bakery.

Estelle knew this because she was a consultant to the School Board, hired to address problems of integrating children whose parents were raised in the villages of the sub-continent into the Ontario school system. What did you do about prayers, for example, and the Christmas pageant?

Anna Ghupta had been living with relatives in the farm-house behind Hi-way Burger, where she worked as a waitress. She had just finished high school. It was after an end-of-school party in a farmer's field that she disappeared, three years ago.

"Her aunt and uncle were disappointed," said Solicitor Howe. "She had given up the traditional ways. They had no control. Everyone knew her, because everyone visits the Hi-way Burger."

Solicitor Howe told Estelle and Harold these details as they stood in the field, looking down at the patch of bare gravel where the body had lain. He poked at the ground with his umbrella. "This is the sort of affair the papers love," he said. "They will say we are racists, devil-worshippers, who knows what. It was bad enough at the time."

The rumour then was that Anna Ghupta had been pregnant. The police concluded only that she had been drinking. Perhaps she fell off the bridge. Perhaps she jumped. Young Willie Dixon and his friends had been at the field party, but they had nothing to say to the police. Yes, most likely she jumped.

"Any idea why they put her here?" said Estelle.

Solicitor Howe shrugged. He wore his customary blue suit. A truck sped by, making speech momentarily impossible. When the truck passed, he said, "High grass by the side of the road where the vandals could toss her from the back of a pick-up. That's what I'd say."

That night Estelle lay next to Harold listening to a storm rage. Sheet lightening flashed across the walls. She felt certain the Dixons were involved, that Harold knew something.

"They say the body came from Trinity United," said Hildy. "They do. That's where she was buried. Place up the Tenth Side Road, no regular services." Hildy knew every road in the county.

Estelle often found herself in the kitchen talking to Hildy. It was not what she had imagined for herself, before she was married.

"How do you know it was a pick-up truck?"

"What everyone says," said Hildy.

"And why," said Estelle, "why would anyone dig up a corpse, after everything's over and done with?"

"Those boys been drinking at the Dominion Hotel, driving around. Plus she was a foreigner. Maybe they don't want no East Indian in the Trinity United graveyard."

"Hildy!" said Estelle.

Hildy stopped talking, but not because of Estelle's scolding. Following her gaze, Estelle saw the white Cadillac in the drive. The Sikh gentlemen alighted.

"Mrs. Macnab. I am S.J. Singh."

He had had a sing-song British accent ("the most cultivated voice I ever heard," Estelle told Hannah). Mr. Singh snapped his heels. Estelle was aware that she and Hildy were staring.

"Wilson," she said. "Ms. Wilson, not Mrs. Macnab."

"Not Mrs. Macnab? Excellent! Quite the nicest news I've heard all day." Mr. Singh flashed a brilliant smile. Estelle did not correct him. "Please excuse my car. Terribly vulgar. I wanted something large, and it was all they had. The seats are scarlet, made of something called velour. Can you imagine?"

She could smell Mr. Singh's after-shave. His eyes were soft. She imagined his grey beard would be soft as well.

"You are surprised," said Mr. Singh. "I see it in your eyes. Let me put your mind at rest. I have come to take charge, to see that the body is properly cremated—what should have been done in the first place."

Estelle invited him to the front room and asked Hildy to bring them coffee. Hildy gave her a look. The front room was never used and Hildy was not the maid.

"It is so refreshing to be here in the country," said Mr. Singh. "In Ottawa, I had dinner with your Prime Minister." He waved a hand to show it meant nothing to him. "The man was positively beGuccied!"

Hildy entered with the coffee. Her cut-off shorts were tight and she wore a halter top. Mr. Singh twirled the end of his moustache. When she had left the room he said, "Rather plump. I like that in a woman."

Estelle smirked (how was one supposed to respond?), but she was affronted. Mr. Singh smiled again, gold glittered in his mouth.

"How did you end up here, in this backwater, of all places, Miss Wilson?" He had appraised her: her bearing, her dress, the sapphire necklace she wore. She must have looked surprised.

"Come, my dear, you are a city mouse, as I am myself. It takes one to know one," said Mr. Singh. "You were not raised here, I am certain. Those sapphires—brilliant!" He leaned forward as though he were going to touch them, but did not. "Is there family money?"

Estelle's forebears had been respectable: civil servants, school teachers, farmers. All but one famous uncle who had come down from the Grand River valley and set up as a whole-sale fruit merchant. Soon he had a warehouse on Front Street. The business prospered. He bought a Rolls Royce with a stove in the back to keep the passengers warm. He died in the Rolls in the company of his mistress, a farm girl from Penetanguishene, and she was dressed in furs. The sapphire necklace, never out of its box, was supposed to have been for this woman, but when Estelle's uncle died, it was discovered and spirited away without her aunt ever knowing. Estelle wore it often; it made her feel proper and reckless all at the same time.

"A little," said Estelle, fingering the necklace. "There was a little money."

"Excellent!"

"Tell me about the district," said Mr. Singh. "And then you will show me the field where the thing was discovered. The daughter of my niece, you see."

A warm wind blew across the field. Mr. Singh viewed the patch of ground for some moments without saying a word. Estelle watched him. The royal blue turban he wore, the matching striped necktie, the carefully groomed beard, his perfect bearing: it put her in mind of a military man, some dashing officer on the Northwest Frontier. She stood straighter, aware of her own robust figure. Foolish woman!

Mr. Singh said, "I will be here for a week or two, at least until they release the body. I am trying to find out what happened, some news for her poor mother, you understand. Perhaps you will help me, show me around the district. I would be so glad of your company." He kissed her hand, a thing no one had done before. They would meet for lunch at the bakery in town the following day.

Estelle learned that Mr. Singh had a house in New Delhi on half an acre of land, that he had servants and gardens and a pond with exotic flowers. He travelled extensively, advising foreign firms that wished to invest in India. He spoke several languages.

"Do you go to Paris?" she asked.

"Often. I work for our embassy there in an informal way. Economics and foreign trade, that sort of thing."

"Do you go to the cafes?" she asked.

"More or less all the time," said Mr. Singh.

Sometimes, at dusk, when she was driving home, Estelle would imagine evenings in foreign cities, the cafés and restaurants filling with people.

He showed her photographs: the dusty plains, rivers, elephants, the white and red palaces of Rajastan, the temple at Amritsar.

He told her he had been married three times, widowed once, divorced twice. Estelle had been married once, shortly after university, a disaster that had lasted less than two years. She had been single for over ten years when she met Harold Macnab.

"Harold Macnab is all very well," her friend Hannah had said. "But with him you're missing the boat. You know it, and I know it."

"He's the only boat there is," Estelle had replied.

"A strong woman like you should have babies," said Mr. Singh over coffee. He winked, put his hand on her knee; he was willing to do his duty. By then she had grown used to his remarks. She had also grown used to the idea that the intimate lunches were leading somewhere, but she did not admit this to herself. The warm afternoons stretched before them as Mr. Singh paid the bill. They had drunk an entire bottle of wine. She felt his knee pressing against her own, his hand brushing her thigh. He mentioned his room at The Highwayman. The conversation turned to the subject of the corpse.

"Why do you think they did it?" said Mr. Singh.

"Religious reasons perhaps?" said Estelle. "Maybe they think a Hindu doesn't belong in a Christian cemetery."

"Surely people do not take their religion as seriously as all that," said Mr. Singh. "I understand they have a difficult time even keeping these country churches open. They have it wrong anyway. She was not Hindu. She was a Sikh."

She told him the rumours, about the boys at the party.

"Those poor fellows," he said. "They will spend their whole lives returning to this incident at the bridge after the party, whatever it was, reliving it, trying to get it right."

Estelle arrived home at five, having accompanied Mr. Singh to the graveyard at Trinity United. She was putting her house keys on the hook above the sink when she heard a truck—Harold Dixon's pick-up, young Willie at the wheel. She saw Hildy get out of the passenger side. Harold came across the yard from the barn. There was a short conversation between Harold and Willie, Hildy standing by. Then Willie left.

After supper, Harold said, "You don't want to get your Indian friend too worked up."

"Worked up?" said Estelle, somewhat alarmed.

"Driving around the country as he is, asking questions; it's a thing that will not bear close investigation." Harold had a thin, gothic face that made her feel she was being judged. And for what? They looked at each other for a moment in silence. Harold said, "The Dixons are family. What's past is past. We will be living here for years and years—you, me, Hildy, Willie Dixon—long after Mr. Singh has gone back to wherever he came from."

When Mr. Singh next telephoned, Estelle was almost breathless. She realized she had arrived at a decision.

Estelle had never been to The Highwayman Motor Lodge. The dining room had black and maroon panelling and the effect on a summer's day was gloomy. They decided to lunch on club sandwiches by the swimming pool. They left the table before the coffee came, more out of nervousness than impatience.

Mr. Singh's room was on the second story and the door lead to an outside balcony which faced the intersection of the highway and the Eighth Line. Estelle imagined people in their cars at the traffic lights observing a middle-aged employee of the school board and a Sikh in a linen suit and blue turban climbing the stairs and walking quickly along the balcony. She kept her face to the wall as Mr. Singh fumbled for the keys.

"Well," said Mr. Singh, inside the room, "here we are."

The scent of his aftershave was almost overpowering, a sweet, heavy smell that Estelle would remember her whole life. She noticed for the first time a certain puffiness around his eyes. Through the window behind him, Estelle could see the fields of Hills County rolling toward the Escarpment. He kissed her. And then he was undressing. Estelle was surprised to see that instead of singlet and underwear, underneath his suit, Mr. Singh wore a kind of short cotton nightdress. When he raised his arms up to unwrap his turban, she glimpsed his penis, old and grey. And beneath the turban was a thin cotton bandanna, done up in a topnotch, like Aunt Jemimah.

Mr. Singh was a man of the world. Estelle discovered she was not a woman of the world. But it was too late, and she did her best. This is how some people behave, she thought to herself, fingering her sapphires afterwards—people in novels, in history, my own great uncle. She wept for only a moment—for Harold Macnab, for poor Anna Ghupta, for what had been lost, for the poor human heart. Then she lay in silence, staring at the beige ceiling, as Mr. Singh began to snore.

Three days later, Solicitor Howe telephoned to inform

Harold Macnab that there would be no further investigations. The matter was closed; the culprits were unknown. The body of Anna Ghupta was signed over by the authorities in Toronto to Mr. Singh. He arranged for a service at a temple in Downsview, whence the remains were taken to a crematorium.

The plain coffin in which the body had been shipped from the pathologist's office was placed on a sliding metal tray. The fire, stoked to three hundred degrees, disposed of the desiccated corpse in twenty minutes, an hour and a half less than the process normally took. Then the fire was out, and there was nothing left but white, powdery ash. That evening, Mr. Singh took the seven o'clock flight to London.

It was August, the hottest day of a wet summer. Estelle was already tired from the heat, and a little wilted. There was a lushness, a shimmering green to the fields this morning that was otherworldly, like Ireland perhaps, but more tropical. In the garden the tomato plants were bent double, heavy with fat red fruit. She could see down into the valley, and the different shades of green there.

But she was not thinking of these things spread before her eyes like a feast. She saw instead the oily surfaces of torpid rivers, dusty palms and wide white streets.

Were people never happy with what they had?

RUDE GROWTH

❖ ❖ ❖ ❖

The Havelock's farm: abandoned. The Applewood's farm on Sucker Creek: abandoned. The Applewood's other farm house—the place near the cattle slough where the hired hand used to stay: abandoned. It had three small rooms downstairs, three small rooms upstairs, unpainted on the outside. When we were children we called it the black house, because the boards had turned black, and we were afraid to go near it. We made monsters of whatever poor drifter or "new Canadian" Mr. Applewood might have staying there. Those were the years before he gave up having a hired hand, before he gave up growing oats and hay altogether.

Mrs. Applewood and Donny moved into the black house the year after Mr. Applewood was killed by a falling willow. That was the same year poor Mrs. Applewood stopped being cultivated, stopped "putting on airs" and become a little queer, not quite right in the head. The truth was the people of Merrick Bay preferred her that way. They sympathized. They understood going a little queer after seeing your husband crushed to death beneath a tree better than they understood putting on airs.

The black house tilted so much it looked drunk. It was unbelievable it was still standing, how it could endure even a gentle wind, if ever wind came to this shallow valley.

"It's hard to believe there is anyone left to come to your meetings," I said to my aunt, driving past the empty house. "Where did they all go?"

Close to the lake, the roads in summer were choked with traffic. Weekend boating made swimming in Merrick Bay virtually impossible. After the beginning of August, people were advised not to drink the lake water because of E-coli: seepage from people's septic tanks. Development along, and immediately behind, the lake was becoming denser and denser every year. Some real estate agents were even hungrily starting to call Merrick Bay "an all season resort community."

And yet here, just a couple of miles back, the land was emptying out, like Saskatchewan. The roads through the country behind the lakes were dotted with abandoned houses, collapsing barns, derelict sheds and chicken coops, and in the fields—what fields there were between the stands of forest and granite outcrops—rusting ploughs and harrows, and the relentless march of weedy trees, saplings sprouting where once there had been pastures for cows and sheep.

"The children leave, the old ones die," my aunt said.

How different she was from my mother, who had been flighty, nervous, given even as an adult to blushing and sudden hysterical laughter. Aunt Beth and my father were in many ways a better match. It should not have surprised me as much as it did that they had lived together under the same roof for longer than my father and mother had ever been married.

I had come home to bury my father.

Aunt Beth rolled the window down an inch or two. The interior of the car smelled of hot plastic. Morning in mid-June, a warm day, and already the countryside looked like high summer.

I was driving my aunt to the meeting of the Women's Institute. It was in the next township; several local branches had amalgamated in response to declining membership. The younger generation in the organization were women of about sixty. But my aunt wasn't concerned that the W.I might wither and die. That was the way of things.

After I dropped her off at the community centre (the building sat curiously alone at the side of the road, no other building within sight) I doubled back the way we had come.

The Allen place. "Don't go near it," my parents would warn me, amazed at how far eleven year olds could travel on their bicycles, how far up the creek we could get in the green punt or on our home-made rafts. The barn might fall down. The floors might be rotten. There might be abandoned wells—you'd fall deep into the darkness and never get out. There was dangerous old machinery, rusty barbed-wire fences. And strangers. Tramps from the freight trains. People who went there to drink. They threw bottles through the windows and shat on the floors. On the trampled grass outside the Allen house, next to an old mattress someone had dragged outside, I examined the first condom I had ever seen. "For protection from disease only."

The Allen house was one of the places where Bert was supposed to have stayed, during the years when he was on the lam from the police. Motorcycle gangs went there. Drifters.

Low women and white trash. And now Donny Applewood, moving deeper and deeper into the countryside, lived at the Allen place; he had gotten it for next to nothing and made it habitable.

I drove by the entrance on the first pass. The front field was completely grown over so that the house, a quarter of a mile back from the road, was hidden from view. An iron gate hung permanently half-open, its lower end embedded in baked mud. The driveway—two deep ruts with a hump of high weeds in the middle—curved around the gate and then followed a gentler curve between two rows of dead elms to the farm yard.

In the high grass around the property were the skeletal hulks of wrecked cars and trucks. There were small piles of tires, doors, fenders, bumpers. And an old stove and fridge. The inevitable dogs prowled the hard-packed dirt directly in front of the house, but these dogs were less fearsome than fearful. They reminded me of the craven half-dead dogs you saw in Mexico, or in the poor villages of the Caribbean.

The house was faded white with robin's egg blue trim. One of the two windows on either side of the front door was covered with blotchy cardboard. The front door was shut, a dirty curtain across the window. There was no sign of life, and the approach to the house, through overgrown with raspberry bushes, was somehow foreboding. I stepped from the car and slammed the door. The only sound was the drone of insects.

I called out. "Hello. Anybody home?"

The dogs approached, abject, base, sniffing my legs and shoes, cowering back in the weeds when I moved. Around the side of the house I found a couple of pick-ups in what appeared to be working order (both had current license plates) and a float, a flat aluminum boat with an airplane engine mounted on the back. These were used for crossing the swamps and muskeg.

I smelled smoke and heard a noise, a hammering, from somewhere behind the house. The lane continued on behind the house, past the ruins of the barn, helter-skelter timbers atop a pile of rock and broken mortar, through a grove of thirty foot sumacs, and into a low dip, what must have once been some kind of gravel pit. Here the collection of ruined cars was breathtaking; there must have been thirty of them, most of them twenty years old or more. In the midst of this graveyard, beside a shack, a rusty forge, and a welding tank, Donny Applewood pounded a piece of glowing metal with a hammer.

"Donny," I called out, "Donny Applewood?"

He turned. His face, though seamed, was still sallow beneath his dirty baseball cap. He was still skinny, except for his arms, which were sinewed with muscle.

He was expressionless. There was no sign of recognition.

"Ray Carrier," I said. "I used to live at the river farm house." I held out my hand. He wiped his on his pant leg. It was like shaking hands with an old shoe.

"I was in Merrick Bay for my father's funeral," I said.

"I heard," said Donny. He pulled out a pack of Exports and lit up, offered me one. The cigarette was strong and unfiltered, and the first few puffs made me dizzy. I looked around and felt I was in a foreign country.

"I saw your mother," I said.

He nodded.

"She was a client, a friend of my father's. Nice place she's

114

in, the Lodge."

"Don't get down there much," said Donny. He motioned to the yard. The smoke from our cigarettes rose to the brilliant blue sky.

"I was hoping—I'd like to talk to your sister," I said. He just stood there staring at me. "You have her address?"

"Why?" he said.

"I wanted to talk to her. Ask her a few questions."

"What questions?"

"Well, you know, my father, they found him at the edge of the bay with an old rowboat. I don't know if you'd remember—it was a rowboat that used to belong to one of the summer families, the Millers, out on Connecticut Island?"

Donny would have been about twenty the year I slept with Quentin Miller. My first love. She'd leave the old boat by the mouth of the creek and I'd row out to the island. We would lie on the pine needles beneath the stars, oblivious, blind.

"We'll look after it," her brother had said later. Then the rowboat vanished, and the Millers went away.

Donny scraped a fleck of tobacco from a tooth with his fingernail and spat on the ground.

"You know, your mother, your step-mother, she used to work out there at the Millers' island. I was hoping she might be able to tell me something about it—why my father had been so interested in that boat. That's why I went down to the Lodge—but your mother..." I hesitated.

"Her mind's gone," said Donny.

"Right. So I figured maybe Marj could tell me something. You know, mother, daughter, they were pretty close, weren't they? They talk. And your sister, she knew Quentin Miller."

He considered. Then he said, "Why're you so interested in all this. You ain't trying to make trouble?"

"I won't make trouble. I'm just trying to find out...well, what happened. My father died. I hadn't seen him for years. I paused for a moment and asked, "So, what ever happened to Bert Latroppe?"

"In the penitentiary for a time. Kingston. Him and Spook—that Indian—Parry Sound way. They killed some guy in a fight. Spook died in jail."

"What about Bert?"

"Kinda lost track of old Bert. Out west somewheres. British Columbia, last I heard."

He threw his cigarette on the ground and picked up the welding torch. From his pocket he took a flint lighter. Without looking up he said, "You go up to the house, get Mary Lou to give you Marj's address. Tell her I said so."

"Mary Lou?"

"My woman."

"I called when I was up at the house. Nobody answered."

"She's up there alright. Got a friend visiting, you must have seen the truck when you came in. Just pound at the back door. We don't use the front no more."

He lowered his goggles and flared the torch. I walked back up the lane to the house. I banged on the back door. It was opened almost immediately.

"Hello, I was down talking to Donny...."

"I know. We seen you from the window. We seen your car come up."

"My name's Ray Carrier."

"We know who you are."

I explained about Marj's address.

"Come on in. I'll get it."

The smell was overpowering, a damp sweetness, clothing and old food, the windows could not have been opened all winter. And it was hot. Despite the temperature outside, the wood stove in the corner burned; it was where they did their cooking.

I accepted a cup of tea. Mary Lou rummaged around in an old secretary desk, while her friend, sitting at the big table with a cup of tea, looked on. She was a large woman. She twined a bit of hair in her fingers like a girl. She smiled at me, and there was something vaguely familiar in that smile.

Mary Lou found what she was looking for. She stood up with an envelope in her hand. She tore off the flap from the envelope and handed it to me.

"There you are."

M. Wilson, I read. The return address, in Cambridge, Ontario, was written in black ink.

"Sorry to hear about your dad. Clare here was just telling me. Funeral was up at the old church at the crossroads, eh?"

I nodded. The jungle telegraph. I was amazed.

"So's your aunt gonna stay on at the house?"

"I should think so." I drained the last of my tea. "Thanks for the tea, the address. I should be on my way."

The two of them followed me to the door. At the bottom of the steps I turned to say goodbye. But Mary Lou was turned towards the other woman, whispering. Mary Lou nodded at her friend. Could it be Clarrisa, the girl from the general store, hidden under twenty years? Mary Lou came striding down the steps toward me, with purpose.

"Come with me," she said.

I followed her across the yard, to an overgrown path through a stand of aspen and young maples.

"Where are we going?" I asked her.

"Going to show you something. Don't tell Donny."

We tramped across a still muddy field in the direction of the old railway line. When I was a boy we used to crouch beneath the overpass, waiting patiently (two trains daily) for it to thunder across, inches above our head. There were no trains now. There weren't even any tracks; the railway companies had torn them up. We walked along the embankment. The ground was low and damp here. In the distance I saw the glitter of sun on water. Soon we were surrounded by swampland. Through the muskeg and dwarf pines, the poles of long dead trees pointed at odd angles toward the sky. We walked in silence, the rude growth swishing and catching at our ankles. I listened for the distant whistle of the train.

"There," she said, pointing to a kind of island, a patch of higher, flat ground in the middle of the muskeg. "They buried it out there."

"What?" I asked. When we were children, I used to imagine that this whole, poor countryside was haunted, and I saw now that it was.

"The baby. Donny and Bert, they put it there."

I was dizzy.

"Some fishermen found it," she said. "Looking for bait, frogs and crayfish and such. Only flat dry place, so naturally they headed for it. Was in a shallow grave, with some other garbage. Stupid thing for them to do. Animals had got into it, I guess. Anyway, they found it."

We stood there on the curve of the embankment of the abandoned railroad, staring at that spot in the muskeg, the sun beating down on us, listening to the sound of frogs and insects and the whistle of the phantom train.

SWEET JANE

◇　◇　◇　◇

I read about Jane's death on the Monday, probably the same day you did, the day you telephoned. Though I'm surprised there was anything at all in the newspapers out there. I thought there would have been only local interest. A "local poet and dancer," that's what the newspapers here said. There was just the one book of poetry, after all, plus a few stories in literary journals, only one of which I ever came across. And the dancing was "exotic." It's not as though she had been with the ballet.

Yes, I do know a few more details than those that were reported in the papers, which I'll tell you. Doubtless there are other details, and rumours of details—you seem to have heard some of them yourself, even two thousand miles away—but I don't move in those sorts of circles. I don't know a single person, now, who knew Jane, or even anyone who has known her over the years.

When her book came out last year, my own name was in the papers for the first time in my life. There has been some small interest in me again, because many of her poems were about me, because she had once loved me, and, because, in an interview, she spoke my name. She once loved me.

You told me once that I was handsome, beautiful. I was shocked hearing that from a man, but now I see it was true, that we were all beautiful: you, me, Keith, Sweet Jane. There were others, hundreds of others, thousands, all around the world. But even then, Jane was younger than we were, golden-haired.

What is my life like now? Oh, I still teach English at the technical college—now they call themselves a university—the job I took to tide me over until my film was finished. I work mostly at home. I look out the window to a long lawn and ancient maple trees and, beyond that, a small ravine choked with rude growth. We know it's not the Rocky Mountains here, but we imagine the city to be famous for its small ravines, underground streams and rivers, its hidden (some would say repressed) depths. I can still hear the echo of my children's voices from somewhere behind me, although I have the house mostly to myself now. The children are gone, one at university, one moved out, down east, in the grip of the name-less rage of youth. I know you don't have children, and that you won't understand these things.

Elizabeth is at work. She is a partner in a large accounting firm. An accountant—I can hear you laughing. I would have laughed myself once.

I haven't been near our old street in twenty years, except perhaps to go to a café or to accompany Elizabeth when she visits design stores. The warehouse Jane and I lived in is abandoned, a little too far out yet to have been carried aloft by the new stadium. Development is spreading along King

Street like a disease.

I remember the time I came home and found you there. You were standing by my bureau going through my drawer, the one where I kept the silk underwear that Jane bought for me and that I never wore. You were fingering the flakes of acid that I never took. I suppose that's what you had been looking for. You never said. Jane was upstairs in the studio, her footsteps echoing on the wide boards above us. It was the middle of the afternoon. Later, I thought about that—about the time of day.

You thought I was naive. But late at night, when she was sleeping, I used to go to Jane's studio and search for needles. She kept them in the drawer with her stockings and underwear. I would throw them on the floor and smash them, while Jane slept in the next room or danced in the bar where she worked. I didn't think I would ever be involved in that kind of thing— that my life would be like that.

Blind perhaps. Stolid. But not naive.

You were still playing piano in cafés and student hangouts. You had your place on Niagara street. My heart was broken, but I thought you would rescue her, and when she went with you to Vancouver, and them to Armstrong, I imagined myself happy—an altruist. You were taking her away from those dirty streets. (Remember the ice in winter, how black it was on the roads and sidewalks, the wind coming off the lake?)

The interior of British Columbia. How exotic that sounded. I imagined green valleys and lakes, dirt roads through forests, meadows with wild flowers, and in the distance the mountains, always the mountains. In the summers you both planted trees.

Perhaps, like me, you imagined a new future for her. I have

a picture somewhere, I know exactly where—in a plastic bag—with her letters written on pale blue paper. In the picture you're both tanned, strong. Jane has her hand to her mouth, about to brush a wisp of blond hair that has fallen across her face, the mountains in the background. Everything clear. Who sent me that picture?

You were the one who introduced her to those things: marijuana and hashish cured in opium, unnameable sorts of hallucinogenics, the needles. You betrayed me. Even months, years later, I was shocked by your intimacy. The first time I visited you at Niagara Street after Jane had moved in, I saw a tiny ball of blond hair on the shelf in the hall landing. Jane's pubic hair. You had shaved her. I imagined you both high and giggling. And then?

Andy Warhol was in town; he was supposed to show up later, and you had asked me to a party. I didn't stay.

She was in love with you from the beginning, of course. We both were.

But you're interested in more recent details. Here's one: the house where she was living when she died belonged to a man called Marino who owned several bars and strip clubs. That was in the paper, that's probably why the story was in the news in the first place. Mr. Marino has "links with organized crime." He's a short, dumpy man with long black hair. There are photos of him stepping from a long white car with tinted windows. She was his companion. Did you know that? First Keith, then me, then you. Then, who knows? And, at the end, Mr. Marino.

Did you hear about Keith? He's given up his job at the University of Michigan to return to rock and roll. His wife has left him. He's in New York, a place off Canal Street. It's not normal. But I envy him. He was here last year and we went to a bar, got quite drunk. A place featuring "European style table dancing." Jane was still dancing in those kinds of places then. She would have been forty.

She used to massage me, massage my whole body, even my feet. Do you remember her hands?

Last year, when the poems came out, I wondered if perhaps you were not just a little jealous. Were you jealous? I know there was the one where my penis was a flower—my wife had a good laugh about that—but the rest were love poems. She didn't mention you in the interview.

I saw Jane for the last time a year ago tonight, the longest day of the year, the summer solstice. I had met a friend for a drink downtown, and we were walking home, up Bay Street. She didn't look as I had remembered. She looked her age. She had a snaggle-toothed, common law husband, wearing blue jeans. He had bad breath and was more a hanger-on or a pimp than a husband, years older than she was. She looked distracted. She made me think that I had, after all, made a life for myself. She didn't look sought after or desired. Now she's dead, an overdose of cocaine, and a blow to the skull.

I wonder, will we ever again be sought after and desired?

The short stories she published, did I mention those? Quite strange: men licking woman's shoes and the like. Some people find this arousing, I suppose.

They found her in a warehouse on River Street, near the lakefront. "Foul play has not been ruled out." That's how the papers put it. She'd been there at least a week. I have a friend, a lawyer with the Crown Attorney's office, and he tells me that there was an injury to the head; that's what she died from, not the drugs. Her head was caved in. Possibly she fell. Possibly she was struck. I have my own theory. I'll come to that.

The house where she lived on Dufferin Street, near the outskirts of the city, belonged to Mr. Marino.

When I met her on Bay Street, she mentioned Mr. Marino. She was thinking of giving up stripping and had heard about a job as manager at one of his fancy restaurants. The Palais. Perhaps you've heard of it?

When she went to see about the job, he brought her into the restaurant to sit with him at a table of heavies. Later he took her for a ride in his long, white car and made her a proposition. It was not the proposition she minded (she had long since slipped into corruption) so much as the risk. What would happen when she left?

Her poems were about me (they were, weren't they?) but the stories seemed to be about the kind of life she led after you left her.

Now the police have visited my discreet house, massive men, whose thick black shoes left a smell in the room.

Why did they come here? Because there were more poems. They had learned of the first "slim volume." They found out who those poems were about, and they knocked on my door. They didn't leer—not quite. There were more stories too, it turned out, stories about the proclivities of a man like Mr. Marino. Shocking, I must tell you. They supposed Mr. Marino did not want such stories printed. She had found a respectable publisher apparently.

"This woman has connected you to this other world," my

wife said this morning. "I think you're pleased to have this in your past." My wife is a confident woman for whom Jane is nothing but a name, but there was an edge to her voice. And in a way what she said was true. I'm not so blind as to miss that. Everyone likes to think that, while others may be bloodless, they themselves are filled with passion.

"Still," she added, "wasn't *she* the one who betrayed you as much as he did?"

Rooming houses, needles, stripping and the paraphernalia of "the sex business" (as though it were just another industry, like auto parts). I think she wanted out and it wasn't allowed; that's my theory.

You gave up drugs, I heard that. You have a good business, I understand, planting trees, a contractor to two provincial governments and several forest companies. You have a house on Galliano. Acquaintances of my wife have rented it.

We escaped and I can't help thinking it was only right that we did.

Still, I do not forgive you.

A SMALL WHITE CARD

◇ ◇ ◇ ◇

"I suppose you want some money."

Mr. Drummond stood by the dining room table with a glass in one hand and a decanter in the other. It was peculiar of Scottish design, emblazoned with a stag, rampant, upon a doe—some obscure regimental joke from Mr. Drummond's war-torn past.

He held the glass up to the light of the chandelier, examined the decanter with his good eye, and measured out the whisky with one deft pour. Exactly an ounce and a quarter—Paul had once checked. Mr. Drummond put the stopper back and returned the decanter to its secret place between the sherry and the brandy on the silver tray, behind a grotesque potted plant and the silver tea service where you couldn't see it unless you were looking. Mrs. Drummond's family was Methodist. She had grown used to having liquor in the house, but still thought it vile to have bottles on display. She hid them as best she could. The vodka was kept in a squat bottle under a tea cosy.

"Just as well," said Mr. Drummond. "The man's a

poltroon, a flatulent blowhard, a communist, a Frenchman, a Catholic—I have no doubt a drug addict."

Paul understood that his father had changed topics and was speaking now of the Prime Minister. Paul had never been able to convince his father that he was not an associate and confidant of that exalted person. Mr. Drummond believed that Paul was intimately involved with the inner workings of the cabinet, and that he ought to share the blame. It would have made no difference even had Paul been able to acquaint his father with the modest dimensions of the part he actually played, for Mr. Drummond held that anyone who worked for the govern-ment was implicated (as he put it), that the whole system was infected with the grandiose, even lunatic personal ambitions of the leader—the man had taken to making obscene gestures at the voters—and tainted by the system of patronage and graft through which whatever party it was had clawed its way to power. They were all equally corrupt as far as he was concerned. Like the Roman Catholic Church.

"I heard the Minister of Finance at the Empire Club the other day," Mr. Drummond said, suddenly turning on Paul like a viper. "What d'you think of that?"

"Well," said Paul.

"Ha! What about these interest rates? Did you have anything to do with that? What?"

"Interest rates are the responsibility of the central bank."

"The central bank? The central bank? Do you want to know what I think about the central bank?"

"What?" said Paul.

"I think they ought to put the governor of the central bank in jail."

Mr. Drummond was mellowing. It used to be that he wanted the governor's entrails torn from his living body, roasted over an open fire, then fed to maddened pigs. Mind you, this was 1981, and the prime lending rate was approaching twenty percent.

Paul's mother came down the stairs. She wore a long blue skirt. She always dressed formally for dinner; she was part of an anachronistic, beautifully turned-out, and tiny minority. She took both Paul's hands and kissed him carefully on the cheek.

"Hello, dear," she said. "How was your trip? Are you awfully tired?" She floated past him to the Madame Récamier.

"Why are they making this Irishman an ambassador?" Mr. Drummond said. "I never cared much for the Irish, though I do love potatoes." He cast a quick eye at Mrs. Drummond. "With the exception of your mother's family, of course."

"It was a good trip," Paul said to his mother. "I left early and stopped off at the Hadley's farm, but no one was there." To his father, he said, "I don't know why they're appointing him. Probably a political matter. They decide these things at private meetings, over breakfast at the Château Laurier."

Paul's mother said, "Did you know that the Hadley girl— Winifred, is it?—has left her husband? They were living in London, and she flew to Paris, never came back. The younger brother, Graham, has written a book—awfully vulgar, I believe. Mr. Hadley is in British Columbia, skiing. The mother is dead, no doubt the result of finally drying out."

"The Château Laurier?" said Mr. Drummond. He turned to his wife. "They run this country from the lobby of a French hotel. That is why I spent six years fighting Hitler." He went to get himself more whisky.

"Andrea has left her husband?" said Paul. He was thrilled. He was transported.

"And you've left your job," said Mrs. Drummond. "What will you do now?"

"I am going to Paris," said Paul, deciding on the spot.

"I was in France once, in 1937." Mrs. Drummond gazed past Paul, out the bay window. "With my cousins. My aunt took us all for a month. It was awfully hot. Then we went to Germany. We all stuck close to my aunt because she had such a tiny nose. No one could mistake her for a Jew." Here she paused. "You often hear people saying that nobody knew what was going on in Germany then, you know—with the Jews. Well it's not true. Everyone knew perfectly well what was going on, they simply didn't like to mention it. We were quite frightened. Europe, it's never what you expect."

Then, turning back to Paul, "Why Paris?"

"Because my youth is passing. One day I shall die."

"Oh dear, I hope not."

"The French," said his father, returning to his chair. "You know what happened in the war. They folded like a cheap suit-case. You ought to go to London. You can get a good suit there. Give you the name of a reasonable fellow in Highgate."

"He won't need a good suit," said Mrs.. Drummond gloomily. "He is going to die."

"I am going to study French," said Paul. "Such a beautiful language. It will be good for my career."

This stopped the conversation. Paul's parents were dumb-founded. Paul had studied French for years at school without sign of any special feeling for the subject. He had no ear for language and, now that he had resigned his job, he had no career either.

But it was what they spoke in Paris. Paul wanted to be as far away as possible from Ontario, and from the bond markets, and from those hallways the colour of urine, where people of Paul's acquaintance spoke—under the glare of fluorescent lights—of how much they would be making per year once the inflation adjustments came through. He had missed something. His vision was filled with these images: he wanted to be at the Dome, the Coupole, the Selecte, the Rotonde, the Flore and the Lipp Brasserie, sipping espresso and wine on the terraces under the peeling plain trees; he wanted to spend languid afternoons sitting beside the pond in the Luxembourg, recovering from nights of excess. He wanted to stroll by glittering yellow domes and the murky green waters of the Seine. Perhaps, after some months, there would be a slim volume of poetry. (He had once published a poem in his school magazine, *The Old Pine Cone*, some rather pretty couplets about a fellow who commits suicide in the spring.) He had read what John Glassco had written, that "half of man's miseries result from an insufficiency of leisure, gourmand-ise, and sexual gratification during the years from seventeen to twenty. This is what makes so many people tyrannical, bitter, foolish, grasping and ill-natured after years of discretion and have come to understand they have wasted their irreplaceable years in the pursuit of education, security, reputation and petty advancement."

Seventeen to twenty? Paul was almost thirty. He had already spent far too much of his life in the pursuit of education, security, reputation and advancement, and he did not want to become any more foolish and ill-natured than he already was. It might already be too late. Cigarettes in the morning now gave him a headache and his knees became sore if he walked more than several blocks. (These were the Drummond knees—what had caused his grandmother to remark in her nineties that she was tired of life.) His youth was wasting away. He had missed Paris. He had missed Andrea Hadley.

"French? What? Study French? What on earth for?" said Mr. Drummond. "How old are you? Almost thirty? When I was thirty I had finished putting myself through law school. Damn." He looked down at his finger. "Got a bad nail here."

"A hangnail," said Mrs. Drummond to Paul when his father had left the room. "It's worse than the time he had the sore foot."

In the dark panelled dining room there was a dinner of fish with spinach and boiled potatoes. There was no salt or butter, and no wine.

"This is a meal which is good for my heart and your mother's bowels," Mr. Drummond remarked. He then said the grace in Gaelic.

It was a rule of Mrs. Drummond's that politics, business and money not be discussed at the dinner table, so conversation was desultory. Mrs. Drummond asked what she was to do with the accumulation of books, papers and old furniture that had recently arrived from Ottawa, Paul's things, and would it be alright if she gave them to the poor? Paul said yes, it would be alright, if the poor wanted them. As far he was concerned he never wanted to see the stuff again. Mr. Drummond said that perhaps some of the papers which Paul had sent home could be used in some way to bring down the government, that would be nice, but Mrs. Drummond said that was politics and changed the subject.

After dinner his father took Paul into the upstairs study and shut the door. On the shelves on either side of the fireplace there were books of history, titles such as Ontario and the First World War, The Valley of the Six Nations, two volumes on the town of York, one covering the period 1793 to 1813 and the other the years 1815 to 1834. You had to have an acute interest. There was a complete set of Walter Scott. On the wall above the chesterfield where Paul sat were pictures of soldiers in full dress uniform, one from each of the Highland Regiments. Mr. Drummond sat in the armchair in the corner—his customary spot—beneath a ceremonial dirk on the wall.

"You know we had to go to Scotland to get a new minister? Porker, I mean Parker, myself, the whole damn search committee. The fellow is almost seven feet tall. Plays the pipes. Still, you'd think we'd be able to produce enough ministers in this country, wouldn't you?" His father paused, eyeing Paul. "Have you ever considered the ministry?"

"No," said Paul. "If I had wanted to be a minister, I wouldn't have studied economics."

It was ground they had covered before. The truth was that in his private heart Mr. Drummond saw himself as a minister—not that he was particularly religious; he simply would have liked to lecture people on the pointlessness of secular institutions and the need for careful accounting, both financial and moral. He was an anarchist himself, but he loved to see order and purpose in other people's lives.

"Porker says they need someone out at the school. Teach history and economics or something. You're an economist, you say?"

"Yes," said Paul. A further pause.

"I suppose this Paris business means you won't be coming up to the lake this summer." Mr. Drummond leaned forward in his chair. "Alright then, supposing we don't put the Minett in the water at all!"

Mr. Drummond glared at Paul, waiting to see what reaction this awful possibility would have. The Minett was a kind of boat, a motor-launch, built in 1935 for Paul's grandfather. It was the sum of all his worldly assets and had come into the Drummond family when grandfather died. It was a very temperamental machine, one of the bloody inanimate things that plagued that family. Mr. Drummond was trying to have the boat viewed as Paul's responsibility. Paul said nothing. A judicious move. His father changed the tone and became agreeable.

"We are always concerned, your mother and I, about your welfare." He had a way of referring to Paul's mother during these discussions which made her sound like a distant and saintly personage, someone with whom they were both only vaguely acquainted. "Do you know anyone in Paris?"

"One or two people. Andrew Cernak. He is a painter. Miles Montrifax who works at the embassy. My friend Max Willis is there now."

"Max Willis?" said Mr. Drummond, brightening. "Short fellow? Has a moustache? Father was with the Dominion Bank?"

"Yes, a lawyer."

"I never knew any Frenchmen myself," said Mr. Drummond. "Knew a German once, some kind of relation of ours. His name was MacTavish. No one ever mentioned him, of course. You have money? If you need anything, let me know."

Mr. Drummond took from his wallet a small white card on which were printed the telephone, address and cable number of his office, and gave it to Paul, the first time in the entire twenty-nine years they had known each other that he had had occasion to do so.

COUP D'ETAT

◇ ◇ ◇ ◇

For months there had been grumblings at police head-quarters, complaints that the government was doing little to stop the training of malcontents in the hills, that the Americans were unhappy. Rumours of unauthorized purchases by the army—even some helicopters (which someone claimed to have seen in crates at the harbour). We discounted the rumours. They were the subject of less discussion in the office than the Deputy Minister's hobbies, particularly those involving his executive assistant, a ripe young person who, it was said, had been runner-up to Miss Philadelphia during her days as a student in the United States. Now there was something you could believe.

As to the rebels in the hills, my wife and I had come across them only once. It was a Saturday. We were out for a picnic. So were the rebels—as far as we could tell. The leader was a slight man of about nineteen, one of the cab drivers who worked out of the Saint George Hotel. I had often seen him lounging against his van in the plaza, smoking and talking with the other drivers. He lent me a bottle-opener and gave me a mango to share with Maria.

"Thank you," I said. "Long live the Revolution."

He was armed with a stick—a stout, sharpened stick, to be sure, but a stick all the same. It was hard to believe that the army could be concerned.

"Perhaps," said Rinaldo, my colleague at the office, "but, from small beginnings...remember Ché."

I did not need to be reminded. As well as working together, Rinaldo and I were co-members of an economics discussion group. The idea was to read and talk about the latest books and articles from the U.S and England. It was a way of keeping up, despite the palm trees. Rinaldo was always trying to push the discussion towards politics. He even went so far as to occasionally wear a bandanna. I believed that such behaviour could do nothing but harm his career, although I never actually mentioned this to him.

"Ché lived in a dictatorship," I said. "I thought this sort of government was exactly what you and your friends wanted. What next—a Peoples' Democratic Republic?"

Rinaldo said nothing. He had been strongly in favour of the Coalition. In fact, at first there had been much enthusiasm for the new government, but that had dissipated. Now there was bickering amongst the members of the cabinet. A lot of clucking by the Americans. Exports rotting at the harbour in clouds of fruit flies. Worst of all, no tourists. Rinaldo could see as well as I could that the thing wasn't working. We both had our careers to think of, and under the Coalition the Ministry was in a mess.

"Where's that report?" I asked, rather sharply. "Fishboy wants to see it."

A report on the development of an air freight service, an attempt by the government to breathe life back into our foreign trade. Fishboy's chapter had been finished for weeks, and he and I were now waiting for Rinaldo. We were all in the running for Section Head, an appointment about which there was much speculation throughout the Ministry.

"Fishboy will get the job," said Rinaldo. "He sucks up the best. Always running upstairs to see the Deputy, memos to the minister. Plus the Englishman likes him." Rinaldo almost spat as he said this. Like most nationalists, he was xenophobic.

The Englishman (Harbottle was his name) had originally come to the country to sell Fizzies, a kind of tablet which, when dropped into a glass of water, produced an effervescent orange drink unpleasantly reminiscent of fruit salts. The product had not been a success. All the same, Harbottle had been able to gull the government into believing he was an expert on trade matters. He was our boss.

"No one in the Ministry except Harbottle likes Fishboy," I said. "Carolina does the best work."

"A woman?" said Rinaldo. "They will never give Section Head to a woman."

Rinaldo had a point. The Coalition may have been left-wing, but they were also Latin, very macho. Both my wife and I secretly believed that this strengthened my own chances of getting the job.

But I said to Rinaldo: "You think we're living in the age of chivalry? The Coalition wants to help women, Rinaldo. You ought to know that. They want to liberate women. They want to liberate everyone."

"But that particular woman is a fascist. If it comes to

politics, I ought to get the job," he said.

"Unfortunately, it will not come to politics. Your position on U.S. imperialism and the International Monetary Fund will not matter to the interview board."

"At least I *have* a position," said Rinaldo, with a sneer. "Not like you. The perfect bureaucrat."

Rinaldo could be rather shrill at times. I believed that his political stance could only work against him; the government, after all, was trying to project an image of moderation. I did not mention this to Rinaldo.

The change of government occurred at two o'clock the following Tuesday. The Cabinet was lunching in the banquet room of the Saint George Hotel on the occasion of the anniversary of their first year in office, when General Diaz arrived and announced that henceforth they would be relieved of their duties. He graciously offered to arrange transportation to the airport for those who wanted it, and suggested that those who chose to remain in the country—and, of course, they would be welcome—should stay in their homes for the next few days, where, for their own safety, they would be guarded by men with sub-machine guns until things returned to a state of normalcy.

Some guards at the Palace, surprised when soldiers arrived in armoured vehicles, had panicked and drawn their revolvers. One man was critically wounded. (It was this which attracted the attention of the international press corps, before they were escorted out of the country.) People were advised to stay off the streets, to keep to their houses. There was sporadic shooting throughout the afternoon, most of it in joyous celebration.

"These are difficult days," said General Diaz. "What is needed is a firm hand, resolve, a sense of national purpose and reconciliation. Together, we can look forward to a time of peace, of prosperity, above all, of order. The hour of our destiny is at hand!"

We heard this on the radio in Carolina's office, late in the afternoon. The broadcasting facilities had been seized immediately.

"The hour of our destiny? A bit much, don't you think?" I said.

"Our Lord Jesus Christ in heaven!" said Rinaldo. "What about the men in the hills? What will happen? They're finished."

"Just the opposite," I said. "At last they have an enemy. The best possible thing that could have happened to them."

The national anthem was played. Carolina's eyes glistened. Fishboy came into the room, rustling papers which he held in his hand. His glasses glittered under the fluorescent lights. Speaking loudly to make himself heard above the stirring music on the radio, he asked about the report.

At five o'clock, two army helicopters flew over the plaza. Jeeps and a tank rumbled on the pavement below, and soldiers with rifles slung from their shoulders patrolled beneath the arcades of the capital.

It was soon announced that, as a result of the excesses and inefficiencies of the previous regime, economic renewal would be the highest priority of the new government. The nation would re-enter the world of international trade. General Diaz himself, in addition to his presidential duties, would assume responsibility for Trade and Development, a great honour for the Ministry. Our Section would be particularly affected. Certainly this was my wife's view, based both on my daily reports of what was happening at the Ministry and on her own sources of information at the tennis club. We were responsible for exports and special import licenses. Within a week there had been orders for several Mercedes Benzs for the new cabinet, but so far nothing else.

A question frequently asked was, "Are the Americans coming back?" Yes, they were. They would buy our produce. They would sell us small computers and software. Also automatic rifles, the first of which were said to be already on the way. This was something about which the Americans wished to remain discreet. Selling weapons to a military coup to put down popular insurrection: it would not be difficult for the enemies of the regime to cast the policy in an unfavourable light.

There was even talk of going ahead with the air freight scheme—bad news for Rinaldo, for he had never finished his part of the report and it had come to light. Things were not going well for Rinaldo. General Diaz had terminated the Peoples' Education Office, through which the Ministry had proselytised in the countryside about the need for true self-sufficiency. The new government didn't believe in that sort of thing. It was a project in which Rinaldo had taken a special interest.

Also, there would be no more gatherings of our discussion

group. Regis Debray had been scheduled for the next meeting. We though it just as well to dispense with that.

"Is that all?" my wife asked when I reported all this to her. "No promotions?"

A devout Catholic and the reason for my coming to this country, Maria is not spiritual when it comes to those elements of the material world which fall within her immediate ken. She had been expecting much from the upheavals in the capital.

"They left the Englishman in charge?" she said. "That means Fishboy will get Section Head. And you, with all your bloody degrees."

It was true: they had left Harbottle in as ADM. Very few officials had as yet been ousted. But the structures which Harbottle had so carefully put in place, the titles and positions— Section Head, Director, Assistant Deputy Minister—all seemed not to matter as much as before. The government had placed a certain Captain Gonzales in the Ministry. He was there whenever the Minister—a white-haired former ambassador to the U.S. who had been brought out of retirement—held a meeting, signed a memo, or spoke on the telephone. The "Liaison Officer." That was Captain Gonzales' title.

"The same Captain Gonzales who plays tennis?" asked my wife, brightening. She leaned forward in her chaise, indicating that I might mix her another drink. "He comes from a very old family." She seemed to think it was a good sign. Maria has an instinct for these things.

One morning Fishboy came to my cubicle with a message from the switchboard. He was excited. He did not, as a rule, bring me my telephone messages.

"The Liaison Officer wants to see you, Mortimer.

Immediately. Chop, chop."

Captain Gonzales was on the seventh floor, the highest in the building, where the Minister and the Deputy Minister had their offices. I saw that the Minister was not in when I reported to the officer at the reception area. This was not surprising because the Minister usually came to work for only two or three hours a day. But the Deputy's office was empty. The room had been cleared out.

Captain Gonzales rose and came around from behind his desk to introduce himself when I was ushered in. Very charming. Very polished. Like the Sam Browne belt he wore.

"Mr. Mortimer. I am so glad you were able to come and see me. You are busy?" His manners were what Harbottle referred to as "continental."

"Things are picking up," I said.

"You have a very important job. It's a very important ministry. There is much opportunity for a man like yourself. Especially now."

He offered me a little cigar from a silver case on his desk. Cuban. The man was broad-minded.

"You know, we are hoping for more exports in the future. Not only our traditional products, but industrial exports as well. Manufactured goods."

I nodded. I was in agreement with whatever the new government had in mind. It was a matter of principle with me.

"For these new products, we will need new factories. New machines. We will need investment from abroad. We do not have enough money in this country to finance our own development. Forgive me, Mr. Mortimer, I don't suppose any of this is new to someone with an education from—where was it?"

"The London School of Economics," I said.

"The LSE, yes. My brother was there. Perhaps you knew him? No, I think not. He is older, with our central bank. As I was saying, investors in our country want some assurances. They are not going to be happy if we have riots in the plaza, like we had last summer. Or rebels in the countryside. Investors are like old women—very nervous."

I nodded. We both chuckled.

"And we will be buying more from the Americans," Captain Gonzales continued. "Materials vital to the well-being of the nation. We will need aid. But the Americans will be reluctant to help if there are bandits in the hills. I think you have encountered some of them. You were on a picnic?"

"You mean the fellows from the hotel?" I was taken aback. Did he also know about the economics discussion group? The office had grown suddenly warm. "That was nothing," I said. "Boys with sticks."

"The hotel?" He took up his pen and wrote something down. He was poised to write more. "Which hotel?"

"I thought I had seen one of them before at one of the tourist hotels. I don't remember which one exactly."

"Perhaps it will come to you later," said Captain Gonzales.

"Perhaps."

"Also, there is a man in your unit, Rinaldo. What can you tell me of him?"

"Nothing." I said, perhaps a little too quickly. I shrugged and added. "A good worker."

Captain Gonzales' gaze remain fixed. "Keep an eye out, will you, Mr. Mortimer? Tell me anything you hear of that might—how shall I put it—discourage investment in our country."

He stood up to show me out. He was smiling again.

"By the way," I said, "where is the Deputy-Minister?"

"He has left the country," said Captain Gonzales, "with his executive assistant."

"Where did they go?"

"Philadelphia. My kindest regards to your wife." He closed the door.

I was back in my cubicle only a moment when the large head of Harbottle appeared above the frosted glass of the partition. It was unusual for him to visit; normally, we were summoned.

"Good morning." He crossed the small space in front of my desk and stood gazing out the window, his hands behind his back. He was upset. Captain Gonzales had reached straight down to me. A break in the chain of command. The whole system was starting to crumble.

"So," he said. "You have met our Captain Gonzales."

"Yes."

"What's he like?"

"Oh, you know—foreign."

One of our little jokes. Harbottle laughed without much amusement. "And what did you two chat about?"

"Oh, nothing really," I said. "This and that. You know. Tennis."

"Tennis?"

"It appears that he plays at the same club as my wife."

"Ah. Yes." He turned to the window. "You know, Mortimer, governments come and go. But we— the professionals, the civil service—we remain."

"Do you think this government will go?" I asked.

He didn't answer that one. Instead he said, "I have been here many years, and I can tell you it is not a good idea to become identified with a particular regime." He turned at the door as he was leaving. "Could be bad for one's career."

◇　◇　◇　◇

"I see. A very tricky situation," said Maria. We were drinking our evening cooler on the terrace. The air was filled with the rich scent of the white star jasmine. "The Deputy is gone. Captain Gonzales is running the Ministry. It is good that he likes you. But the Englishman is still in charge—he will pick Section Head. There's no getting away from that."

"Right, my dear, as always. On the other hand, if Captain Gonzales were to become annoyed with me, well...."

"But you can't go telling him things about Rinaldo, *spying*," said Maria. "At the convent, we were always taught that sort of thing is simply not done."

"Quite right, my angel. But as of this afternoon, there will be nothing to tell about Rinaldo. Rinaldo has resigned. The man has his principles."

"One down," said my wife. "What about the woman, Carolina?"

"She has the right politics. But they have a conventional view towards the role of women, the army. Fishboy remains the obstacle."

Maria placed her empty glass on the arm of her chair where I would notice it. She considered it bad manners for a lady to ask for—or indeed have anything to do with—the business of drinks. I rose and mixed her a fresh one at the glass table by the wall.

"With a big slice of lime, just the way you like it," I said, handing her the glass. Unlike most people, Maria has never lost her taste for cuba libre. "By the way, my darling, did you by any chance happen to mention to any of your friends at the tennis club about that time in the hills?"

"Time in the hills? What are you talking about?"

"The picnic last summer, when we come across those fellows training, armed to the teeth with sticks."

"I do not remember."

I will say this about Maria: she is a very ambitious woman. She gives me the confidence to do what must be done.

Two weeks later I received a message from Rinaldo asking if we could meet. I left the office early and strolled around to the Saint George. Rinaldo and I met there frequently. The meetings of the economics discussion group used to be held in the downstairs bar. They made a particularly good frozen daiquiri. When I arrived, Rinaldo had already ordered his. He seemed rather intense, even for him.

"What about the automatic rifles? From the Americans."

"Rifles? I don't know anything about any rifles," I said.

"We know for a fact the weapons are coming," Rinaldo said. "From Miami. We know that the Ministry is handling it. All I need to know from you is when. The date and the hour."

"From me?" I glanced around the downstairs bar of the

Saint George Hotel—at the limp artificial palms in their immense pots, at the high barred windows. I was struck by what a sinister looking place it really was.

"Is this a good spot to be discussing this sort of thing?" I asked. "They have been asking about you. I hope we haven't been seen. I am still hoping to get Section Head."

An unpleasant expression crossed Rinaldo's face. "I came in through the kitchen. You do not have to worry. We are safe here. We will be warned if anyone is coming."

This was worse than I had expected. Anyone capable of warning Rinaldo that the police were coming would also be capable of telling the shadowy officials in the basement of the Ministry of Justice that I had met with him.

"I know nothing about the rifles," I told him.

"Perhaps you can find out. The man who sells cold drinks from the cart in front of the Ministry. Tell him. He will get the message to me."

Rinaldo turned and left through the kitchen doors. I ordered another daiquiri, then a third. Then I returned to the Ministry, now empty. I ascended to the sixth floor, to Harbottle's office. I took the precaution of using the fire stairs rather than the elevator.

There was no oily charm the second time I was called into Captain Gonzales' office. I remained standing while he addressed me from behind his desk.

"You know that we have been expecting guns." I gaped in a way that I hoped conveyed puzzlement. "At the insistence of the Americans, the transaction was being handled by a civilian agency. I am speaking, of course, of the Ministry."

"The Ministry?" I rasped. "Guns?"

"They arrived last night. At the small airstrip north of the city. I am sure you know the place. It is not used much. That is why it was selected. But nobody was there to meet the airplane. No one from the Ministry. No one from the army. No one from the police. No one. It appears we had the wrong night." Captain Gonzales glared at me. "The pilot waited. He noticed men approaching in the darkness but was unable to take-off in time. The men disappeared into the trees with the cargo. By now the weapons are doubtless in the hands of rebels through-out the country."

"I suppose the thieves had been watching the airstrip," I suggested.

"You don't think someone could have tipped them off?"

"I very much doubt it."

As to the actual arrangements for the shipment, making certain that the plane was met when it landed and so on, well, I told him, I really couldn't say. That wasn't my responsibility. "Just a foul-up, I'm afraid. There have been mistakes before. Very unfortunate."

"Who was in charge of this operation?"

"I'm not really sure," I said. "I think Mr. Harbottle may be able to help you there."

I arrived home early with a chilled bottle of champagne. Maria was in the garden reading a paperback novel by Graham Greene.

"Good news," I said, "I have been promoted."

She rose from the chaise lounge. "Section Head at last,"

149

she said.

"Not Section Head."

"What, you mean Director?"

"Try again."

"You mean—ADM!"

"In an acting capacity only, but still."

"My darling! But what happened to the Englishman?"

"Gone. Not clear where. England I think. Fishboy will be leaving too."

"You sit down," said Maria. "This time *I* will get the drinks!"

General Diaz has drawn up a new constitution with a promise of free democratic elections three years hence. I expect that at that time I will vote Social Democrat, or perhaps even for the Front. I would expect a thorough shake-up of the administration, during which I might be confirmed as an ADM. Of course, if the Front comes to power, Rinaldo will certainly be a senior member of the Cabinet, and I would hope to make Deputy. In the mean-time, I've assured Captain Gonzales there will be no more foul-ups with the air freight service.

ARRIVAL

◇ ◇ ◇ ◇

I came to the islands because I longed for the exotic. I wanted to be some place else, to descend like a diver into a different world.

Once I met a man from Kent, in England, and for him it was the clear cold north, not the north he knew—Leeds and Bradford. He yearned for another kind of north, an empty place of ice and tundra, himself in skins and furs. He wanted to go to Baffin Island. Baffin Island? I'd been as far as Smooth Rock Falls, I told him. It seemed to take all day, and once you got there you wanted out, to head south again.

I wanted another kind of island, with palm trees in a southern sea. Nothing would be the same. I thought people changed by leaving things behind. There would be mild weather and possibilities, languid women on the white sand, dark rum with knobbly limes and oranges. Maybe, in the back-ground (quite far back), someone with a gun—a hint of dark romance. And everywhere you looked the radiant silhouette of palms against a brilliant sky.

But I was not a castaway. A person has to eat, so the bank

paid for the move. Relocation allowance, it was called, but really it was just a perk, a scam. Karen said it was a joke, said it with a sneer. In her eyes I had somehow grown corrupt.

I stood on the pier at dusk waiting for the ferry. The air had suddenly turned cool. Across the channel I could see the steady wink of the Pigeon Cay lighthouse, a rhythmic ten and two. Summer in the West Indies, but the sea was the milky green of Lake Huron in the fall. Behind me Healey chattered into the pay phone.

Earlier that afternoon, the plane had touched down at some flat place in the Berry Islands and left me on the runway. A message had crackled over the radio about engine failure, someone stranded. As we began our descent, I saw a patch-work airstrip, surrounded by scrub bush. Down low the land looked like the Canadian Shield, like a place I flew into once north of Bancroft. Karen had just joined the band and was doing a tour of dingy bars in northern and eastern Ontario. Sometimes, on a Saturday, I would fly up to join them. Karen was always on about her gigs. I hated that word, I used to make fun of it. It sounded like appendages, I said—or a bunch of one-night stands, which turned out to be closer to the truth. Karen said I was just a banker. I was doing mostly loans to car dealers then.

We bumped, then taxied to a stop near some abandoned tractors. The equipment was shot through with rust, the blue and white airline insignia eaten away by the salt air. By the edge of the runway an old DC3 sat half shrouded in brown canvas, ropes anchoring the wings to the ground. One of the engine cowlings lay in the weeds. A boy with an oily rag in his back pocket gazed into the motor.

The pilot opened the door of our plane. A blast of hot wind rushed through the cabin—a smell of oil and the sea. I stepped onto the tarmac. I'd been travelling since six that morning, with only a couple of hours at Miami, time enough for three bloody Marys. The alcohol, the long hours, the hot sun: I was drugged.

Near the squat metal terminal a man in white trousers and a pale blue shirt spoke to a black woman. He held a clipboard. "It's criminal, absolutely criminal," he said. "She should be with her parents." Next to him stood a woman with a wailing child in her arms. Our pilot came out of the terminal. He looked harassed. He turned to me and said, "Mr. Rennison?"

I nodded.

"Okay for you to wait here a while? Get another plane, maybe an hour from now?"

You could tell from the tone of his voice that he didn't want an argument. He squinted at the sun.

"We've got a kid here who's real sick," he said. "She can sit on her mother's knee but we're still short one seat. You're the last name on the list...." His voice trailed off and he shrugged.

He said I could use the radio-phone in the terminal to call Healey.

"How will I be getting out?" I asked.

"Plane over there," he said, pointing to the DC3. I must have looked surprised, because he touched me on the shoulder and added, "She's in great shape."

In five minutes they were gone. I stood alone at the outdoor loading area, drinking a warm soda from the Coke machine, a 1950's model. I sent a message to Healey.

Perhaps an hour later I was awakened by a jeep skidding to a stop. The driver was lanky, sun-burned and wore silver-framed, mirror glasses.

"I'm your pilot. Bob Wade."

He took a duffel bag from the back of the jeep and we walked to the DC3. A van pulled away.

I sat in a jerry-built seat behind the pilot, the wall of the cargo compartment close. The boy with the rag in his pocket jammed my luggage in and climbed into the co-pilot's seat.

"Don't usually carry passengers," Wade said. "This is the best we can do."

"What do you carry?" I asked.

Wade didn't answer. He said, "We put down at Marsh Harbour. Then you take a boat."

As he spoke, I looked down. A gun slid from under Wade's seat so that it lay beneath my feet, dull black, almost camouflaged by plane's metal floor. A long, thin barrel. It was all I could have asked for. I asked about the weather.

"West wind blowing, rain tonight, maybe tomorrow. After that you should get sunshine."

I told him I was with the bank. We were setting up an out-island branch. We had to appear as though we were serving the people here, I said, not just taking their money and sending it to Montreal.

Originally, they'd planned to run the office from one of the other islands. The branch was only going to be open three days a week, maybe more in tourist season. But I'd approached the bank and sold them on the advantages of having someone permanently posted, someone who had worked at head office in Montreal and could help with Caribbean and Latin American country analysis. I knew a little Spanish.

Merton was surprised at the request. He was a hot shot, younger than I was and already on the 22nd floor. My boss. That was another reason I wanted to go.

"It's a job more suited to an older guy, someone on the way out," he said. "What, you got burnout? In your thirties?"

Karen and I were supposed to be living in Montreal by then, but she was still with the band, working out of Toronto. There were long distance phone calls. I wanted her to quit and come home but they were always on the verge of some record contract. I hadn't seen her for weeks.

"What about that lady of yours?" Merton leered. He had seen Karen at some office party. Loose hair, cornflower eyes, open-toed shoes—she had made an impression.

"She thinks it's a great idea," I said.

But Karen stayed in Ontario. It was a choice she'd made long before I came to the islands.

We started our descent. From the window, I saw Healey standing by the chicken wire gate at the edge of the runway. He'd come in from Nassau earlier in the week and was staying with the local agent at Marsh Harbour. Healey was responsible for all four of the out island branches.

The plane shuddered to a stop.

"You need any help?" Wade shouted over the roar of the

engines. I shook my head. I had only a single bag.

"No, I mean at the bank," he yelled. "You going to need any help at the bank?"

This surprised me. "It's possible," I said. "Maybe a teller. I don't know."

He waved. "Yeah, well, you take care now." He pulled the stairs up into the cabin and slammed the door.

Healey wore baggy white slacks which flapped in the wind, white shoes, a vivid blue and green souvenir shirt, and blue aviator glasses. I told him he didn't look like a banker.

"So? It's nearly six. The bank's closed. Welcome to the islands."

Healey was at the bank because his father said he needed experience before joining the family business. They had pulled strings to get him the Caribbean.

"So what took you? I got a taxi waiting. See that fat guy with the beer, whizzing under the fender? That's our driver. Hey, you're going to love the islands."

The vegetation along the road was low and dry. Not green, not tropical, not lurid. We drove by nodes of bleak, cinder-block development—a liquor store, a hardware store, a dentist's office—separated from one another by stretches of russet field and scruffy trees.

"How are things?" I asked Healey. "Ready for business?"

"Ready for business? Christ, what's that supposed to mean? I thought you came down here to get away from the bullshit." I shrugged. "Yeah, everything's set. The walls are painted. We got a counter from Barclay's when they closed. The place is small. One room. You want to embezzle, drink on the job, you've got to go out back. You got a great thing going here—no boss, no work. Not much night life. Still, better to be here than Montreal. All you've got to do is land us some customers."

Healey wasn't surprised when I came south. He knew what had been going on. Karen had met the guy from California by then, the sort of man I wouldn't understand, she said—a poet.

"A poet?" Healey had laughed. "From California? That's classic. I bet he has a ponytail."

When I met Karen she was planning to be a music teacher in primary school—music therapy, actually—and I was with the bank. She said I needed to loosen up, so I smoked a little dope with her once in a while. We were living north of Toronto then, near Newmarket, almost in the country, in the urban shadow where nothing is settled. If you looked south you saw the apartment buildings along Highway 11. To the north were fields of corn. Karen laid out a herb garden and tried making fancy fruit jams. The trouble started when she got into this performance course at night school—all about feelings and relating. She started talking about how she wanted to do more with her life, about how she was going to change. I hated that kind of talk. I didn't understand that then—how a person could want to change.

The taxi took us through town to the ferry-dock. Half an

hour and a sudden rain squall later, we glided into Pigeon Cay harbour by the glow of the running light. The tide was out; we had to watch for sandbars. I could see nothing but the ghostly shapes of sail boats, a dark forest on the far hill and, like a stage set, the jagged outlines of the palm trees.

We climbed the ladder by the hazy light at the end of the pier, then onto a broad and curving path, pale in the darkness, with small houses close by on either side. The air was warm and heavy with the scent of flowers.

"This is the main street," Healey said. He tapped his foot on the sidewalk. "The Queen's fucking Highway."

He had rented a house at the far end of the village where I was to stay until I could make more permanent arrangements. There were no street lights here and the house was dark. We stumbled past the flimsy picket gate and up the path. Inside, there were two beige and orange bedrooms and a living room with a kitchen and a counter in one corner. It was like a suite at the airport Ramada.

On the kitchen counter was a bottle of rum and a white plastic bag of grapefruits. There was a messy misspelled note that read: "Welcome Mr. Rennison. And Bank."

Healey had no idea where it came from. We drank some of the rum, and I showered and went to bed.

The bank was a one-story white clapboard, unkempt bougainvillaea and oleander on either side of the door. The shutters were open; the windows were without glass. The temperature was seventy-nine degrees and would rise as the day wore on. It was almost September, but how could you tell? Healey said you could tell because none of the tourists had arrived yet. He said it was too bad we had to work, because the high proof rum cost only two dollars a bottle and there was great dope, whatever you wanted, down at the Riverside Tavern. He knew the markets like the back of his hand. Healey had an MBA from the Wharton School of Finance.

When I walked into the bank that first morning, Healey was at my desk going through papers from his briefcase, a show of activity.

"Someone here to see you," he said. He nodded in the direction of the bench by the front door.

She was a pale woman, mid to late thirties, in an old blue dress that drooped around her body as though it was melting. She looked to me as though she drank.

"Mr. Rennison," she said. "You got my present?"

Healey stood up. "I'll be over at the hotel having a coffee." He left by the rear door.

"I got your present," I said. "Thank you. Thanks very much."

"Mr. Wade, he's a friend of mine. He told me you was coming."

The ceiling fan turned slowly, stirring her wispy hair. I asked her what she wanted.

"I want to make a deposit."

She handed me a crumpled envelope. I counted out seven hundred and ninety dollars in American and local bills, mostly tens and twenties. I noticed that the money smelled.

"Mr. Wade, he said the bank opening here today, so I come

right over. You want the business Mr. Rennison, right? I got a lot of friends."

I didn't care about her friends, but I took the money.

The hotel next door was called the Majestic. Healey was sitting by the pool—the Terrace Bar—with a couple of beers on the table. "One for you," he said.

He said the woman's name was Annie. She ran a little bar at the other end of the island, toward Tilloo Cay. Not many customers, local fishermen, some of the Haitians who lived in the bush, maybe once in a while big spenders in flashy speed boats from across the channel. She wasn't licensed, but she allowed them to gamble.

I told him about the money.

"Your first customer. Congratulations," he said. "She wouldn't talk to me. How did she know your name?"

"Wade, the pilot. He called her yesterday afternoon."

"Wade runs drugs, you know. That's probably where the money came from. Annie is doing small-time dealing on the side."

"Money is money."

"Oh, absolutely," said Healey. "Absolutely. But not everyone is as broadminded as we are. You don't want to go mentioning this to anyone else in the bank. Or to Montreal."

"She wants me to give her daughter a job," I said. "Fifteen years old. The girl is coming to see me this afternoon."

"We already have someone to work behind the counter. A girl from one of the old white families in the village. It was set up by Nassau—with Burnett's help, of course. Jobs are scarce here. They want to do everything right. Of course, it's up to you."

The island school, a pink-shuttered, gingerbread cottage, was set in a grove of wispy casuarinas at the end of the village, perhaps two hundred yards from the bank. At noon I heard the chiming of the old-fashioned bell.

"Mr...Rennison?" She stood in my doorway, must have run all the way from the school. She wore the school uniform, a blue tunic and white blouse. Her dark hair was in long braids. Tall, slender, pretty. She was mulatto. She looked at her shoes.

"You must be Annie's daughter."

"Yes please, and I would very much like a job here at the bank, Mr. Rennison, sir." She had a small, hesitant voice.

"What's your name?" I asked.

"Azalea."

"A pretty name. Why do you want this job so much? You want to be a banker?"

"No, sir. I want to save money for business college, in Nassau. I'm too old to be going to the school here."

"Well, I'm sorry, Azalea. The job is taken."

She shrugged her shoulders, took the few steps across the room, and placed a piece of paper on my desk before she left. It was a note of recommendation from her teacher, along with her marks. Straight A's.

Another thing: I was expecting the Yacht Club to be wide verandas and faithful servants, stewards in white jackets bringing round the gin on silver trays while the gentlemen played cards and smoked fat cigars—Somerset Maugham country. Instead

161

you brought your own bottle in a paper bag. The convening committee provided mix, ice cubes, plastic tumblers and a sullen black man at a folding table to set them up. That was on Saturday nights; most other days the place was locked up and shuttered tight. The club was nothing more than a wooden hut with a covered stone patio at the side. An overgrown trellis protected members from the gaze of curious passers-by. Across the road in a hut identical, but for the faded paint and whiff of urine, lived a large family of ragged Haitians, refugees who had stumbled from the sea one night.

"Pace yourself," Healey advised, as we strolled along the Queen's Highway. Tonight I would meet Burnett, a failed citrus grower and a member of the bank's board of directors. Healey had been briefing me on the guests. "Don't get drunk until the rest of them do. When the food comes round, go for it because it's gone in a second. Pigs at the trough."

This was one of the summer racing days, so all flags were flying: the Stars and Stripes, the Maple Leaf, the Union Jack.

"Don't look now," Healey whispered as we approached the entrance. "I think we're being followed. Riffraff. Hold on to that bottle."

We passed through the open gate of the trellis and made our way through the little crowd. People were dressed in colourful shorts, oxford-cloth shirts, boat shoes. There were only about thirty people here, but the noise level was rising quickly.

"Where is the bar?"

"First things first," said Healey. "I must introduce you to our fearless leader."

Burnett kept the title of vice-chairman, even though he

spent most of his time in the islands. Occasionally he flew to Montreal and New York for meetings. He was standing in the centre of the room talking with three others, all in their mid to late fifties. He was tall, with a ruddy face—probably as much from the rum as from the sun—and slicked back iron-gray hair. He shook my hand, then introduced me to the others.

"Our new man in the village," he told them.

"Welcome to Pigeon Cay, Mr Rennison," said Mrs. Holborne. She was from Connecticut, yet she had a curiously British accent (the way old money talks, Healey said later). "I can't tell you how happy we are to have a new face at our little club. Especially someone so young. And handsome." She examined me with a vulture's eye. Mrs. Holborne's third marriage had recently ended because of some trouble with a stable manager. She was one of the seasonal residents and did not usually come to the islands until November; on this occasion she was returning home from Lyford Cay, and had stopped in for only the day.

Tom Hargreaves was a balding, ex-foreign service officer, with a flaky sunburned forehead which he scratched habitually. He had a reputation as a sailor. His wife Mary stood beside him, and a foot or so behind. Her movements were quick and bird-like. Her hand when we were introduced was damp.

"These are your future customers, my boy, if you play your cards right," said Burnett.

"Astonish me," said Mrs. Holborne, "and I am yours."

"Don't see why I should switch over from Marsh Harbour," says Tom Hargreaves, scratching his scaly pate.

"Because it will be so much more convenient," said Burnett.

"You made the arrangements to hire Winnie, the girl behind the counter," I said to Burnett.

"I hope you approve. Winnie is a Macdonald. Old family—one of the families who settled Pigeon Cay at the time of the American Revolution. She'll bring you business. The Macdonalds must be related to half the people in the village. Her father is the last dinghy builder on the island."

"These local people are so simple," said Mrs. Holborne, with a wave of her hand. "So charming."

"What would happen if we hired someone else?" I asked.

"Nothing much. Might annoy some of your potential clients, I suppose." Burnett took a sip of his drink and looked at me for several seconds. "It's up to you, of course. But the paperwork and so forth, that's already been done. Bit of a bother to change horses now."

"Besides," said Tom Hargreaves, "Winnie is white."

"How about that drink?" said Healey, bustling.

"I'm with you there," said Tom Hargreaves. He turned to lead us through the crowd the bar. "Steady as she goes."

We gave our orders. The barman paused, mid-drink and looked over our shoulders toward the door.

"What is it?" I asked.

On the sidewalk outside there was shuffling, a scuffle, angry shouting. The vine leaves on the trellis shook. Someone lunged against the gate.

"It's your first customer," Healey said to me.

It was Annie, accompanied by several boys.

"Let's lie low," I said.

More angry shouting.

"Don't let her through," someone yelled.

A small crowd had started to gather outside the Yacht Club—some of the Haitians, some of the villagers, even some of the men from the Riverside Tavern were beginning to drift along the walk towards the Club.

"Are we to be caught in some kind of riot?" said Mrs. Holborne. "How too exciting. I simply cannot believe it!"

"Tom, should we leave?" Mary Hargreaves said, working her hands in front of her.

"Steady as she goes," said Hargreaves, edging toward the rear of the terrace.

A group of men gathered around the door. Through the lattice-work we watched the struggle—Burnett and some of the others were trying to calm Annie. Something flashed in her hand, then the glitter of a bottle tracing an arc through the air. The bottle smashed against the door frame behind me, showering glass at my feet. Dark rum dribbled down my shirt.

"Pigs!" She glared through the fence. The crowd beyond the trellis began to sway and murmur. We faced each other through the vine leaves. At last a couple policemen arrived. One of them tipped his hat to Burnett.

"Alright, then, Annie, come along with me. The rest of you—there's nothing to see. Off you go."

Annie's voice faded as she was lead into the darkness. The sullen crowd dissipated.

"Rennison," said Burnett, returning from the fray. "Do you know what? That dreadful woman out there, she was asking for you."

"Really?"

"Any idea what she wanted?"

"None at all, I'm afraid."

What would happen to Azalea now that she had no job?

"Nothing," Healey said. "She'll wind up hanging around the bar and sleeping with low-lifes on the beach."

I woke late with a headache. I walked across the narrow hump of land to the Atlantic side of the island. In the sky to the south I watched the silver speck of an airplane shimmering in the sunlight until the drone of the engines faded into the rush of the surf. Above me the fronds of the high palms click-clicked in the wind. Something was different, but it wasn't me. It was only these late summer days. How different they were from Ontario—the slamming of the wood screen door, pale dust in the tall grass, the electric buzz of the cicada fading into the afternoon.

HOTEL PARADISO

◇ ◇ ◇ ◇

I lay in a tropical illness. Nausea, cramps, fever: the reaction to the touch of one of the strange plants which grew in the forests behind the village, the poison wood perhaps; or to the hallucinogenic blossoms that flourished, untended, in the lurid garden beneath my window where the banana quits fluttered; or to the dreamy caress of the emerald arms that beckoned from the filtered sunlight of the ocean floor, or to the venom of the sea anemone or another of the tiny spined creatures that lived in the reef.

Or perhaps to the sun. Upon my first arrival at Pigeon Cay, more than two years before, I had taken to the beach and burned my face so badly that my skin exuded a clear, orange liquid for several days. I was treated with ointments and shade, and have since been unable to spend more than brief periods in the sun.

I lay in the living room, the coolest place in the house, and gazed at the green light through the shutter slats, waiting for the weather to break. Ed Holder wanted to bring the doctor over.

But it was only a fight, that's how it began, a fist fight in a bar—no need to bring the doctor in for that sort of thing. Refined Doctor Cutter, trained at McGill, what would she have done but view with disgust a cut lip and those flowers of blood around the eyes? For the first time in two years, I was lonely. I had started to dream about Isobel Cutter. I did not want her to see me like this.

The illness started with a fight, but like an opportunistic virus or an introduced species, it had transformed itself into something else: a kind of melancholy, a new way of seeing. Once, in a dessert campsite in New Mexico, a scorpion bit me. It was like that, the puffiness and fever. I was unhinged.

Or was it merely torpor, those unnaturally hot days? It was late April, but it felt like July. It was the islands, but it felt like the tropics. The weather was freakish, the ocean breezes gone; the only movement of air on the entire island came from the ceiling fans of bars and a few ancient air conditioners.

At Cape Hatteras, eight hundred miles to the north, a storm was gathering, moving eastward, and the seas were starting to build.

It was the weather, but it was also the season; the tourists were gone, the hotels were empty. Most of the expatriates had gone back to Vermont, Connecticut, New York, to country houses in England, in Canada. Later, in the dog days of summer, illegal Haitian workers might come out of the bush or across the channel to repair and renovate, but for now the great ocean-side villas, the pink and pastel green cottages, were shuttered tight.

Later, we might have sailors, real sailors, who navigated their own boats down the coast and across the Gulf Stream, not the millionaires who chartered fantastic yachts in the winter, but for now the lagoon was almost empty. Two of the marinas had closed for the season. Business was flat.

And for some reason the drug trade had abandoned us as well, vanished overnight. For good, we learned later; those entrepreneurs had started flying their light planes straight to Florida, then into Louisiana, Alabama, Texas. They had started sailing their ships up to the Carolinas, to Maine, as far north as Nova Scotia.

Whole days, then a week, then two weeks passed with no one coming into the bank other than Drover, the village storekeeper. I was lonely. I was depressed.

"How did you get into a fight, anyway?" asked Ed. "You're not the kind of guy who would be in a place like that at one o'clock in the morning."

"Jay McInerney," I said. It was a game he played, these references to novels, literary allusions. "Hardly up to your standards, I would've thought. And shouldn't the author be dead? Isn't that the rule?"

"So sorry," said Ed.

"I used to box, when I was at university, at Hart House. I've sparred occasionally with Healey here, on the beach, once even at a gym, over at Marsh Harbour. Tommas somehow knew that."

"Writers who box," said Ed. "Like Hemingway and Fitzgerald."

"Hemingway and Morley Callaghan, you mean; Fitzgerald was the timekeeper. And Tommas doesn't box; he fights. You should have been there. You could have been timekeeper. Where were you?"

"I was in the bush, talking to the Haitians in the refugee settlements."

"Did you find out anything?" I asked.

"No."

"What did I tell you?"

"I know something's going on. They're afraid. That's why they won't talk."

"You talk to Burnett, the fellows at the Yacht Club?" I said.

"They're a bunch of racists just waiting for something to happen," said Ed. "A riot, something."

"*Burmese Days*," I said. "George Orwell."

"So, what were you doing in that bar?"

"Drinking. What else?"

It was between seasons, and we drank. Even some of the Haitians who lived beneath tin roofs and the palmetto leaves of lean-tos, and made a bit of money for their families clearing other people's land, doing odd jobs—you even saw them in the bars. I had never seen Tommas in a bar before.

It was as though we were waiting for something to happen. It was too hot to drink outside at the Terrace Bar, so we drank inside, in the windowless lobby of the Majestic Hotel— they had a species of air conditioner there—or at the Riverside Tavern, built on wooden pilings above the harbour. Through a hole in the floor you could see the pulsating jellyfish which thrived on the sewage. The white sand, the palm trees, the exotic rum drinks, the last gleaming yachts in the lagoon, the visions of nearly naked women on the beach: what did they mean to us now?

Ed said, "Weather like this—it can't last. Something's got to happen."

"Maybe it's an asteroid," I said. "It is heating the earth as it hurtles into the atmosphere, like an exploding sun. We have a day to go before it all ends, day and a half at most."

I lay back on the wicker chesterfield, my arm across my forehead. I could almost see that bursting sun.

"Where's that from?" said Ed. "Not J.G. Ballard. Something by John Wyndham?"

"Rod Serling. *The Twilight Zone*. This guy can't get warm, he's freezing to death. Then he wakes up, looks out the window, sees the sun, getting closer and closer."

Ed Holder was a newspaper reporter from Toronto. He was a little younger than I was, maybe thirty-five. He'd originally been a friend of Karen's. We used to talk about books, but we had never been close. He was a precise person. He was a foreign correspondent, a war reporter really, yet there was never a hair out of place, never a crease or a smudge on his jacket. War correspondents were supposed to suck back the Marlboros, but Ed Holder didn't smoke. He had this way of pursing his lips.

There was something else we had in common, besides Karen and a dilettantish interest in literature. ("That guy's read more books than anyone I've ever met," said Healey. "Is he gay, or what?") We had both fled. We were both refugees, in pursuit of the exotic (the rumour was that Ed lived with a teenage girl in Guatemala City). I had not been glad to see him. I was taken aback when he came into the bank, unannounced. He had been in a camouflage flack jacket, all pockets, and heavy duty shoes.

"You're a walking cliché," I told him. "You've seen too many movies. Read too many books. You look like a war correspondent."

"I *am* a war correspondent."

"Oh? Where is the war in the Bahamas? Let me guess— the drug war. You're hot on the trail of the Medellin Cartel."

"I've come from Haiti."

"You stayed at the Hotel Oloffson, a gingerbread mansion of towers and cupolas. You took dinner on the old verandahs, festooned...."

"Festooned?" said Ed. We had strolled over to the lobby of the Majestic.

"Festooned, absolutely, Don't interrupt, festooned with bougainvillaea, overlooking the unkempt garden, dangerous and foreboding at night. The swimming pool was empty. Perhaps there was a corpse. You drank by yourself in the bar. In the morning, you strolled up to the lush heights above the town, to Petionville, where the corrupt and wealthy live, behind their garden walls, dogs straining on chains. Back at the waterfront, you searched out voodoo—*voudon*, you call it—and were disappointed to learn that visitors are welcome to the ceremonies, that the hotels arrange regular excursions. You strolled through the market, taking in the smells. In the late afternoon, you returned to the Oloffson. You felt cleansed by the tropical rain. You rested before dinner between crisp white sheets. You awoke, refreshed, excited. After dinner and your customary session in the bar, you sat on the verandah in the moonlight, too restless to sleep. You could hardly wait to get into the hills the next day to see the poor, the destruction they've done to their land, and the evil that's been done to them. You wished, somehow, you could be more—committed."

"You've been there?" said Ed.

"Never. But I'm an exile myself. *The Comedians*, by the way. Graham Greene."

"When did you become such an asshole?"

"Oh, it's been a gradual thing."

"Don't you care about those people, the refugees?"

But it wasn't a question of caring. Across the planet people were in motion, millions of them. I knew that. I did "Latin American Country Analysis" for the bank. Thousands of Latin Americans entered North America every day. The flight northward was ceaseless. And it was going on all over the world: in eastern and southern Europe, Mexico and India, in Ethiopia and Somalia, throughout Africa. What did the few hundred Haitians and the fewer Cubans who came here matter next to all that? Even people who were not starving and not being persecuted were on the move. Look at me. Look at Ed.

"Care? Am I a caring person?" I said. "Jesus, Ed. What next? Am I in touch with my feelings?"

"They're individuals, you know. They have names."

"Spare me."

"How long have they been coming here?"

"Years. Centuries. Columbus first, then the rest, looking for the green light."

"You mean the green flash?"

"A myth: there is no green flash at sunset in the sub-tropics,

Ed, so you can stop looking for it. No, I meant the green light at the end of Daisy's dock, the green breast of the new world. They came long before the unfulfilled, dreamy foreign correspondents, arrived with their tropical luggage at the Hotel Oloffson in Port-au-Prince."

I poured myself another drink from the bottle of *ron añejo* the barmen had placed before us. It's true: I was becoming an asshole.

"There's another myth, isn't there, Dave." Dave! How I hated being called Dave. "Even more juvenile than the foreign correspondent. The dissipated expatriate. Humphrey Bogart, maybe? Malcolm Lowry."

"Not Malcolm Lowry—too pathological. Go with Paul Theroux, or Somerset Maugham. He was the original."

"Anyway, it's not the Oloffson I'm interested in," Ed said. It's the Hotel Paradiso."

"Home of monster cockroaches and German tourists. They let them go nude on the beach there. What do you want at the Hotel Paradiso?"

He shrugged, playing things close to the vest. "A story I'm working on."

"A story? Ed, there is no story at the Hotel Paradiso. It's the Riverside Tavern you want. That's where the drug buyers go. Or Annie's Bar. Gambling. Cocaine traders doing business with your Colombians, they drink there. Cigarette boats carry the stuff to Miami. Although you're a little late. But go ahead, go down to Annie's Bar. End of the reef, lee side of the island, can't miss it. Even if you don't find anything for your story, you can get laid. I guarantee it."

That was six steaming days ago.

"Would you like me to bring you anything?" Ed said. "Water? Ginger ale?" I waved him away, and reached over to the basin of cool water on the floor.

"If you'd been there with me, you might have learned something—about the Hotel Paradiso."

"That is what your fight was about?" said Ed.

"Yes, in a way. I think it was."

I sat in the fetid lobby of the Majestic Hotel on the third night of the heat wave. Bottles glowed in the yellow light behind the bar. Red and yellow streamers rippled out from the air conditioner above the doorway. A group of Haitians sat at a table in the corner: Seymour Dufresne who worked as a chef, Ti-Paul from the ferry; and Tommas, Tommas the Poet. He did not live in one of the settlements in the woods, those ramshackle huts of cardboard and plastic sheeting, driftwood and bits of cast off wood and iron. He had a real house, a concrete bungalow on a corner of Burnett's property, in return for which he did a little work around the plantation. Burnett even paid him a wage. Tommas was a Haitian who travelled. He was interested in politics. He wrote and published poetry in three languages. He knew voodoo was nonsense.

The Haitians were drinking Wray and Nephew—clear overproof from Jamaica—the cheapest rum in the bar. Ti-Paul said, "Hey *bass*, business bad?"

I shrugged.

"Least you got a job."

I was starting to hate my desk in the bank overlooking the harbour as much as I had hated my desk in Montreal, and those long grey corridors. But it was true, I had a job, and it would have been churlish to say more.

Seymour said, "How come you never lends us the money? How come, *bass*?"

Seymour was always looking for financing for a salvage operation, refurbishing the cruisers and sail boats that people abandoned or that washed up in the swamp up Black Creek. But who would buy? Not the rich or the drug dealers. They were the ones who had abandoned the boats in the first place. The villagers and the Haitians didn't have money.

I sat at the bar drinking. Tommas was looking at me. He was clean-shaven, short-haired, neat, and intense. He wore gold-rimmed spectacles. He was one of the few on the island who I had thought respected me. When he turned to me, I assumed it would be to talk about writing.

He said, "Haitians don't need money, right *bass*?" He put exaggerated emphasis on the last, a word he never used. "The black man always has *voudon*." The frames of his silver glasses glittered in the yellow light. I could not see his eyes. But there was something in his voice. He said, "You still lending money to those Nazis at the Hotel Paradiso?"

"Norwegians, not Nazis. And it's only a revolving line of credit. Working capital. They repay like clockwork."

"You should give the money directly to us." He pounded himself in the chest, and he hissed as he spoke (quiet unlike him) leaning towards me.

Silence.

Tommas said, "You like to box, *bass*?" Again that unnatural emphasis. "*Bass*, you box, I said?"

"Oh, it's nothing. Used to a do a little. I'm out of practice."

"Do me the honour. Spar with me."

I'd be happy to, I told him. I meant sometime, in the future. But Tommas had risen from his chair. He folded his glasses and put then on the table.

"Here? Now?"

"It would be a great honour." By then I knew that it was not honour he was interested in. I had twenty pounds on him, but I was afraid. He said, "The room is air-conditioned. Why not?"

In boxing I had one move, or sequence of moves: I would guard with my left, jabbing, waiting for the chance to throw an uppercut with my right. It had worked at Hart House and it worked with Healey. But I was flat with Tommas. His big punch was his left. My guard was useless, and I did not know how to adapt. He danced around for a few seconds, snapping at my midriff, then he connected with my right eye. I wobbled, felt warm blood. The room tilted. I jabbed but didn't touch him. There were two more hits, one to my mouth, one to the other eye. Tommas was using both hands. He held his arms low, a sign of contempt. With the final blow, I fell to the floor. It was over in perhaps a minute. I had not hurt him once.

Tommas put on his glasses and left. Vero came around from behind the bar with a towel, helped me to my feet. Seymour and Ti-Paul looked down at me from their table, expressionless, no longer jovial. I was wheezing. The smell of beer and earth and old cigarettes on the floor of that bar—I though I would vomit.

"I'm a little out of practice," I said.

"No shit, Great White Father," said Seymour.

◇ ◇ ◇ ◇

"So it was about the Hotel Paradiso, how you lend to them but not to Seymour Dufresne," said Ed.

"A matter of policy," I said. "At the bank, we have a thing called 'loan criteria.'"

"How does the hotel keep going?" asked Ed.

It was a question I had never asked. People were waiting for someone to develop the Hotel Paradiso, turn it into a Club Med. But there were no buyers. Only those few German tourists. And the bar, where low-end visitors liked to go in hopes of inter-racial sex.

"Is it possible," said Ed, "that you don't apply your 'loan criteria' to European hotel owners in the same way as you do to Haitian refugees?"

"It is possible," I said.

"They have a pier there, at the Hotel Paradiso?"

"They have."

"Freighters dock there?"

"Occasionally. Only place on the island they can tie up, drop off building supplies, minivans and the like. Occasionally the *Violet Mitchell* on its weekly run from West Palm. Others from time to time."

"I think I know how they make their money," said Ed.

"I thought you'd say that. You reporters. Clever."

"Yes, and I've been here what—not quite a week? You've

been here over two years."

On one side of the Hotel Paradiso was a swamp they called Fish Mangrove. Half water, half land, wound through with narrow paths, it was where many of the illegals first came ashore, swimming or dragging small boats into the muck and making their way into the bush under cover of darkness. There were bare foot prints in the clay.

To the south the land rose in sharp coral cliffs. The Hotel itself was set in a perfect half-moon bay, a crescent of white sand fringed by a row of royal palms. Here the sea was still and clear. Angel fish and giant rays swam along the bottom. The pier extended almost to the middle of the bay, so that yachts sailing the passage might stop.

But few did. The shore was jagged with the hulks of derelict cars and trucks and empty oil drums. There was an old bulldozer and a heap of ossified asphalt (someone had once planned to build a go-cart track). The hotel was concrete, streaky grey with a dull blue metal roof. Scattered in the unkempt growth behind were cement block cottages with incongruous thatch roofs. And behind those, a thin stream of smoke from a bonfire.

We approached as the sun sank behind the silhouette of forest. Ed had shamed me into accompanying him. Besides, my health was improving, the nights were cooler, and I could not lie on my chesterfield forever. As we tied the outboard to the pier, we noticed something dark and looming in the dusk of the middle channel. A freight boat, the *MV April Gallagher*.

The proprietor of the Paradiso was a Norwegian named Swan. The captain of the *April Gallagher* was also Norwegian, originally a whaler, who had come to the United States years before. (This was reported later in the Miami papers). They were sitting at a table by an open window in the lounge. They looked up as we walked by. The captain turned to Swan, as though to ask a question.

"It's only my banker," said Swan. "Not come to collect, have you? Join us?"

I declined. There was no air conditioning here. The walls were streaked with moisture.

"Who is your friend?" asked Swan.

"This is Mr. Holder," I said. "A client from Montreal. He's interested in resort properties. May we look around?"

Swan considered a moment. He said, "Is Mr. Holder as discreet as you are?"

"Absolutely."

"Then go ahead. We have only four guests at the moment. Try not to disturb them."

I showed Ed the lounge, the kitchens, the cottages, two of which appeared to be occupied. Then I waited for him on the small rise behind the hotel. People came here to watch the launch of the space shuttles from Cape Canaveral, eighty miles to the west. There would be a pale green flash in the morning sky as the booster rocket burst away.

From the back of the hotel, Ed beckoned me, then called. It was becoming hard to see in the fading light. Nearby, a Haitian worker threw rubbish onto the bonfire.

"Something to show you," Ed said. I followed him around the side to a basement stairwell. He opened one of the wooden doors. Cool, mildewy air wafted up as we descended.

There were perhaps thirty people in the basement. They sat huddled on the dirt floor. I didn't recognized any of them. These were people who had never ventured from the settlements into the village. How long had they been here? How long had they been waiting for passage? None could speak English. A few had suitcases, many had green garbage bags. A young woman held a child in her arms. The basement smelled overpoweringly of urine.

"I grant you, this is peculiar," I said to Ed. I began to sweat. My fever threatened. My eyes hurt. "Let's get out of here."

Outside, clouds moved across the face of the moon. At last a breeze was rising.

Ed asked how long refugees had been on the island. I couldn't tell him. No one had seen the first Haitians disembark and drag themselves through the stinky mud of Fish Mangrove. One day they were simply there. We only knew they worked cheap—a few dollars a day—and that they did work that few others would do: clearing the bush for a new house, a banana plantation, a stand of papayas; quarrying the razor-sharp coral; washing or peeling at the kitchen sinks of resort hotels.

April 20th dawned beautiful, the air cool, the sea calm. The weather and my fever broke. But there was something strange: my house faced the lagoon. The Atlantic was almost half a mile away across the hump of the peninsula, yet I could hear a steady roar. A rage sea was up.

The first reports came crackling over the citizens' band at one in the afternoon. Ed Holder insisted we take the outboard and have a look.

There are two stretches on the Pigeon Cay-South Florida run where ships are at risk—the Gulf Stream and Whale Cay passage. Sailors are prepared for the Gulf Stream. Whale Cay is different. It is the only part of the passage between the islands and the Gulf Stream where ships must enter the open ocean. The rest of the way is protected by the reef and the islands along Little Bahamas Bank. Whale Cay is one of the few places where the offshore reef is interrupted, and the ocean floor rises, so that the channel and the Atlantic Ocean come together in shallow waters, creating the potential for large breaking seas.

There were no buoys, no aids to navigation here. The waves were twenty-five feet high, flecked with foam. We would have to turn back momentarily. Ed shouted at me from the front of the boat, but I could not hear him over the bright roar. Then he pointed. He had his story.

The *April Gallagher* was a hundred and sixty foot long with a twenty-five foot beam and a draft of ten feet, and she wallowed upside down in the main shipping lane at the north end of Whale Cay. The bow remained above the water, brown and splotchy.

Air-Sea Rescue came later and picked up the survivors: the captain and all but one of the crew of six. The rage that day was the result of a build up of water from heavy seas off George's Bank and Cap May, a thousand miles away. It was a surge that moved towards the islands at a speed of over six iundred miles a day, thirty miles an hour. The stern of *April Gallagher* had been lifted out of the water as she came back into the inner passage. Without her rudder, the ship broached and rolled upside down in an instant.

I wondered what they had seen as they sailed north that morning, the air clear, the long green cays shimmering to the east, the small islands to the west low and light compared to the hills of Haiti. They would have seen the turquoise sea, the candy-stripped lighthouse, the pastel villas among the wispy pines, the cut-out of the high palms.

They would have been below, straining to see through the portholes. There would have been silence except for the throb of the engines. In the air, the sea-salt freshness, and a whiff of diesel fumes assuring them that they were steaming north-ward, away from the islands.

Behind the Hotel Paradiso, I walked through the remains of the bonfire: plastic bags and suitcases and ragged clothing which nobody could possibly have wanted. Some old furniture. A television set. They had been allowed to bring one bag each.

I gazed out to sea, towards the green light of West Palm Beach, the Florida Gold Coast, the strip-plaza continent that stretched away from there. I knew what it was that I had been waiting for.